The Plague

Ryan L. Canning

The Plague

tellwell

Tellwell Talent
www.tellwell.ca

ISBN
978-0-2288-2298-1 (Paperback)
978-0-2288-2299-8 (eBook)

I would like to thank my editor Deirdre Madden
for all her hard work helping to shape the
story into the best it could possibly be.
I would also like to thank photographer Annica
Picard for her help in creating the cover.

Photographer: Annica Picard
Model: Lisa Picard
Costume by Ryan L Canning

In the year 2025, a bad flu vaccination caused the death of over 130,000 Americans. Before this mishap, doctors and scientists had already been struggling to prove that vaccinations were in the best interest of society as a whole. A culture of overprescribing antibiotics for many medical conditions that didn't require them, led to antibiotic resistant strains of bacteria which already had many people doubting the effectiveness of current medical practices. Combined with a faked paper and a TV personality promoting pseudoscience, an atmosphere of misinformation had been created. After the incident, there was simply no reasoning with the general public. This mad panic allowed the President to bend the rules, to declare himself president for a third term, telling the public that they needed stability and strong guidance during those pivotal years. The academics knew it was bullshit, but sadly they were the minority. The masses rallied behind their President. They rallied behind him when he outlawed vaccinations, they rallied behind him when he completely revamped the public school system to cut science-based subjects, reduce math requirements, and discouraged any type of higher learning, putting tight restrictions on who could work towards advanced degrees. Many of the lucky candidates were grandfathered if their parents held the same degree. Others were in a type of lottery that was undoubtedly rigged.

The transition into a dictatorship was so subtle, it all started when he invoked plenary power some time in his 4th term. The masses barely noticed until it was too late. Using his new powers, he rewrote the constitution to suit his needs. This new constitution was simply referred to as "the book." After the initial bad batch that killed so many people, many scientists and doctors predicted where society was headed, so they went underground. They did their best to stockpile vaccinations and administer them to as many people as possible. As word got out about the underground, the President expanded the anti-vaccination law. Anyone caught making them, distributing them or administering them were arrested without trial, and the ringleaders of the scientific underground were executed in a very public fashion.

In the very beginning, Britton's parents were a major part of that underground. They used their funeral home to help wherever they could. They stashed materials in caskets and urns, and hid the occasional wanted scientist in caskets, driving them out of town in their hearse. The stakes were high, but as worried as they were for themselves and 10-year-old Britton, they knew the risk was one they had to take. As Britton got older, she also joined the underground. That's where she met her future husband, Todd.

Ten years after that bad batch of vaccinations, diseases that were long thought to have been eradicated were making a comeback on a large scale. It was around that time Britton's parents contracted a disease from one of the bodies in their morgue. Todd took samples from her parents and the cadaver, and went to meet an underground contact, with the hopes of getting them help. He never returned. Britton assumed government agents had caught up with him. There would have been no way to explain away the samples he had with him.

With no way of determining what her parents had, or treating them even if they had known they died just weeks after Todd disappeared. Britton didn't even have the opportunity to tell any of them she was pregnant.

After Hunter was born, with no husband or parents, Britton completely stepped away from the underground, as the risk was too great. She couldn't stand the thought of leaving her newborn without a family.

Year 2045

"Good morning, Doctor."

"Shut up, Adi," Britt said, laughing, "You know I'm still a long way from my Ph.D."

"I know, but that title, 'Doctor', it just fits, you know." Aditya was a tall, handsome man. His parents were ethnically Indian, but they both had been born and raised in London, England. They had immigrated to the United States when he was very young but they never lost their British Accent, one he also picked up. He was very intelligent, with a dry British wit which made him endearing to everyone he met.

Shortly after Hunter was born, Britton had hired Adi to help her with the funeral home. He started off as an apprentice, and quickly became her right-hand man. He helped her with the business and with Hunter. He was her best friend.

He was working absentmindedly, washing a cadaver on his prep table, one of the very few bodies they were able to actually prepare for a funeral. The lucky people who were properly prepared were usually members of the local community that died of non contagious natural causes such as heart attacks, strokes, or accidents. Anyone that died of a contagious disease was put in a cheap cardboard casket and fed right into the furnace.

Adi always brought up Britt's work on her Ph.D., partly to keep her motivated, but he was also very proud of her. She was one of only a handful of people in the world accepted into the Doctorate of Mortuary Sciences program.

"Did you finally pick a thesis subject?" he asked sincerely.

"I think I'm going to do it on old diseases, focusing on the Black Plague."

"Cheery," he said laughing.

"Right?" she said, "at least the President didn't shut down medical school."

"Yet" Adi replied.

Britt took her spot at the second prep table and pulled down the thin white sheet that was covering a man in his 40s.

"The trouble with working here 12 hours a day, spending time with Hunter and then spending a few hours each night working on my thesis, is they are all starting to blend together. I keep seeing signs of the plague everywhere."

"Oh ya?" Adi was starting to cut into the body on his table to prepare it for embalming.

"Ya, like look, this guy's lymph nodes are swollen. It seems to be everywhere, look they're swollen under his arms, his neck, and groin. If I didn't know any better..."

"Oh ya?" he asked again, this time walking over to her table. He looked at the lymph nodes she was pointing to, then he poked a couple with his glove covered hand. "I don't know Britt, I think they look normal, you know, for a body that's been dead for a week."

"Ya, I know, I'm crazy. I just wish the hospitals were allowed to tell us how these people died."

"Me too, it seems like a no-brainer to me, especially with the number of diseases out there now," Adi said. "But I guess they're so busy now, too, and their lab is essentially shut down. They may not even know, either."

"Too true," Britt agreed.

"It's probably just Gonorrhea" he added.

Britt laughed and went on with the task of preparing Mr. Green, her former teacher.

"Honey, get your shoes on, I'm ready to go," Britt yelled to her 10-year-old son who was busy playing a game on his phone.

"Do I have to go?" he asked with a disappointed tone.

"Yes, you do, it'll do you good to get out of the house."

"I go to school every day, how much more out of the house do you want?"

Britton wanted to get angry at him, but she was more amused at how much he sounded like her when she was his age. "Come on, we won't be long, and I'll take you to that restaurant you like."

Their town was small, so their only restaurant choice was a truck stop on the main road. He put on his shoes and was about to walk out of the door.

"Honey, aren't you forgetting something?" she asked.

"Mom, do I have to?"

"Yes, you know the rules."

"Fine," he conceded reluctantly as he put on his respirator mask and gloves. "I look ridiculous."

"No, you look like a young man who doesn't want to get sick and end up in the basement."

Living in a funeral home, death wasn't a taboo subject and they often made jokes about it. Many people found it to be tasteless, but it was the same sort of humour she had grown up with, and her father before her.

Once they were both ready, they hopped in the car and took the 15-minute drive into town. The town consisted of a small general store, a restaurant, and a liquor store. On a Saturday afternoon, many of the town locals hung out in the general store and restaurant, talking about the week's events.

Like in an old Western, when Britt and Hunter walked into the general store, everyone stopped talking and looked at the pair. At one time, the Gravel's were revered members of the community. Her Grandfather had even been mayor. But now, with the distrust in anything to do with science, they were outcasts.

She knew having Hunter wearing a respirator mask and gloves didn't help any, but she preferred to take the dirty glances and gossip over a sick son. She just hated that this was his childhood. She ignored the glances and went about her errands, talking casually to her son about school work and what else he wanted to do that weekend. She was hoping he would say some of his school friends would come over and play, but she knew he was just as much an outcast as she was. This knowledge just motivated her more to make a happy and memorable childhood for him.

After the initial ostracisation, two older women started talking again. Britt overheard one say to the other, "Look at her, not a care in the world, what does she care we're all dying, at least she's getting rich off of it."

Instead of correcting her, which Britt knew was a lost cause, she just continued shopping.

The ladies started talking about the Bangor, Maine flower show. The second woman said, "Oh, dear, didn't you hear?"

"No, hear what?" the first asked, concerned.

"Last night, the entire greenhouse was vandalized. A group of people came in and picked all the roses! The show is going to be canceled this year."

"Oh no, why would someone do that?"

"I do not know, these kids today have no respect for anyone. Especially with all that's going on nowadays, we need something to take our minds off of all the bad things that have been happening."

Britt knew she was talking about all the death, and found it amusing the woman was reluctant to use the word. The woman continued, "I hear they have been hit so bad that they're using the local hockey rink to store all the, well, you know."

"Store the what?" the other woman asked as Britt was walking behind them.

She leaned in and said, "The dead. Bangor is using hockey rinks to store all the dead people, because society has lost their minds and we're not allowed to vaccinate people. Now everyone is dying needlessly."

The two women exchanged displeased glances and walked off in a huff. Britt knew she shouldn't have said anything, especially in front of Hunter, but she couldn't take it back now.

After Britt picked up all her necessities for the week, they went across the street to the only restaurant in town. They were met with the same hesitation and mistrust that they had been in the general store. Once they ordered, Hunter looked at his mom.

"Mom, why do these people hate us? I thought we were trying to help them."

"We are honey, they just don't like our kind of help. They think we're the bad guys."

"But you'd never hurt anyone, Mom."

"I know that, and you know that. One day when you're older and you take over the business, I hope things have changed back to the way we were, and people come to you for help in their time of need but right now, we just keep doing what we do and hope the country survives."

"We were in town earlier. I'm still getting the same warm welcome," Britt told Adi as she started back to work.

"Splendid. Did any of them have anything interesting to say?"

"Not to me, but they did say something about a flower garden being picked clean in Bangor."

"Oh ya? What was the occasion?" Adi asked.

"It wasn't for an occasion, apparently it was an act of vandalism or something," Britt replied.

"Strange indeed. Any word on the people disappearing?"

"People? What people are disappearing? Oh, I hope it's the old ladies at the store."

"You haven't heard?" Adi asked surprised. "It's been all over the news."

"We don't watch a lot of news anymore, it's entirely too depressing. Just more deaths and the incompetent President spewing nonsense, making things worse."

"But sometimes they do come up with something interesting. For example, the missing people. Apparently, many of the sick are disappearing all over the country. There are all kinds of rumours and guesses, from aliens, to ghosts, to secret government agents. I even heard the Canadians were coming down to give the sick free healthcare."

"OOooooOOOO, ghosts, I like it," Britt said with a laugh. "I always thought Canada was planning something, up there being all polite. We're not buying it anymore."

"Right? Look at us, we have a Queen, pip pip and cheerio," Adi said with an even thicker British Accent.

"Wait, you're British, their Queen is your Queen."

"Shut up, I am not," he said with his best American accent.

"Adi, hold on a second. Come take a look at this," Britt said. She was examining the body on her table. As Adi walked over to her, she held up the fingers of the corpse. "What do you see?"

"His fingers are turning black, like frostbite. How long has he been dead?" Adi asked.

"I don't know. Judging by the rest of the body, I would say not more than a few days. It's absolutely not blood pooling. But frostbite?"

"I know, it's not nearly cold enough out. Diabetes? Adi suggested.

"Possibly, but there is no sign of it on his legs or feet, and usually that's the first place you see it. Look, he has swollen lymph nodes too."

"Not the plague theory again?"

"I know, I know. Just humour me. It seems to fit, right? Or am I completely losing my mind?" she asked.

"It couldn't hurt to call the CDC," Adi suggested.

"I don't want to bother the CDC. If the plague was making a comeback, it would have been mentioned somewhere."

"Britt, with the new laws, I assume the CDC is up to their eyeballs and may not have the time to catch new diseases." He paused as they looked at each other and smiled. "You know what I mean, they may not have time to discover all the new diseases making a comeback. New diseases? Old diseases? Whatever. Give them a call."

"That's all the more reason not to call them. They have to be busy."

"I am not saying that this is the plague. But if it is, we need to figure it out and fast. What if that's patient X?" he said, with the flair of a magician revealing a trick.

Laughing, Britt replied "Patient X, in Aurora Maine, out of nowhere? Alright, I'll give them a call, but I probably won't even be able to get through."

The number was on an old list, tacked to a wall. She dialed and left it on speaker phone. The phone didn't even complete a full ring. "Hello, CDC, James speaking."

"Oh wow, I'm sorry, I wasn't really expecting a person to answer so quickly," Britt said, stumbling over her words.

"Ya, well, we don't have a lot going on these days. The Government pretty much seized all our equipment, and there are, like, 5 of us. We mostly watch movies all day." Britt wasn't sure if he was kidding, but judging by the tone in his voice, assumed he wasn't. "So, what can I do for you?"

"I'm calling from a funeral home in Maine."

Before she could finish, James interrupted her. "Oh, a funeral home. That's why you thought we were still around. Most hospitals know not to call us anymore. They're worried the government is monitoring our calls."

"They're not, are they?" Britt asked half-jokingly. She wouldn't have been surprised if a third voice came on the line and said, "No, we're not."

"Who knows anymore, man. Anyway, you were saying?"

"Anyway, I'm calling from a funeral home in Maine. We have a body on the table. We..." She started awkwardly laughing because she realized how absurd she was being. Judging by the huge smirk on Adi's face, he also thought she was crazy, but she powered on. "We have a body on the table and he's got blackened fingers and swollen lymph nodes."

"I thought any swelling like that would shrink after the body dies."

"It usually does. That's why we're a little concerned."

"Oh, sounds like the plague," he said sarcastically.

"Well, funny you should say that..."

"The lymph nodes, are they oozy or are they hard?"

"They're squishy, but we didn't pop one or anything."

"Okay, pop one. If it's gross and oozy, it might be the plague." Britt was surprised by his blasé attitude and non-clinical verbiage. "We are Funeral Directors, we don't really do anything unnecessary to the bodies."

"Good to know, but what is he going to care? He's dead. Go ahead and pop the zit and see what comes out and we'll go from there."

"If I do that, can you guys analyze the fluid?"

"Oh hell no. I don't think we even have a microscope around here anywhere. You're pretty much on your own. Oh, hey, by the way, record it as you do it."

"Oh, would you be able to determine what it is by colour or something?"

"Absolutely not. I just think that it would make a fantastic YouTube video. Have fun, let me know if you've got the plague. I've got to run. Pizza is here."

"Thanks for your help," Britt said, dripping with sarcasm.

"Well, that went well," Adi added after she hung up the call. "So, we doing this or what?"

He stood with scalpel already in hand.

"I guess we are, but do you know what you're looking for? I mean, I have an idea, but the research doesn't really go into how to tell if the ooze is plaguey or not. What is it supposed to look like under the microscope?"

Before Adi could respond, there was a loud knocking on the door, followed by the thunder of several feet walking down the stairs. Britt went to meet them, worried a customer would walk into the morgue. The basement was strictly off-limits to the public, for obvious reasons. Before she made it to the door, it swung open. Several men in suits and respirators barged in. The first man had a piece of paper.

"Hello, I'm looking for whoever is in charge."

Britton walked up to him, "That would be me. You guys can't be down here."

"This is Executive Order 2028-45, it says I can be anywhere I want to be," he said as he pushed past her. "We're just here to do a routine inspection of the premises to make sure there is nothing unlawful going on here."

Adi and Britt exchange worried glances. They both wondered if the phone call to the CDC had actually been tapped, but they knew there would be no possible way they would get there that fast. They also knew, if the men had been 10 minutes later, they would have been caught analyzing the fluids in an attempt to diagnose the man on the table, which they assumed would have been a big no-no. The government agents spent an hour going through everything, all her notes, all her equipment. They went through all the cabinets in the morgue and all the offices, as well as their home. Since it was attached to the funeral home, it was apparently fair game as well. They didn't find anything, but assured her they would be back.

After the excitement of the visit, both Adi and Britton figured they were letting their imaginations get the best of them. There was no way the body on the table had actually died of the plague. They decided to call it a day and finish processing the bodies in the morning.

The next morning began with Hunter sitting at the table eating Fruit Loops and watching TV, while Britt made herself breakfast, and lunch for the both of them. They weren't overly chatty in the mornings. She usually needed a cup of coffee to perk herself up. She wasn't sure what Hunter did to get himself going. He didn't like the taste of coffee, but as soon as he saw the bus coming down the road, he lit up and started to run around like a twitterpated Tasmanian Devil.

While they were watching his cartoons, a preview of the news popped up. They talked about more disappearances and they also cautioned their viewers about a group of miscreants dressing up like plague doctors and scaring people. They cut to a grainy, slightly out of focus clip of a lone plague doctor standing in a field with a low lying fog up to their knees. It was just standing there, staring. She thought it was creepy. She stopped what she was doing to get a closer look at the TV.

"What the..." she quietly said to herself, censoring herself before she finished the thought.

"What is it, Mommy?" Hunter asked.

"Nothing honey, that figure just looks like the men I'm studying in school."

The newscaster equated it to the great clown scare of the mid-2010s. She couldn't wait until Adi got to work to discuss the situation.

As if on cue, there was a knock on the door. The knock was purely for show. Adi was one of the family, so he just walked in without waiting for a response.

"Hey Britt, did you see the…?" He stopped once he saw the TV. "How weird is that? It looks like your crazy plague theory might be true after all."

"Funny guy, but what do you think it is? Some random kids trying to scare people like the news says?"

"I don't know," Adi said, then turned to Hunter. "You better get going mate, I saw your bus on my way here."

"Okay, thanks," Hunter replied as he jumped off his chair, grabbed his bag and ran out the door, leaving a ring of milk on the table and a half eaten bowl of cereal. He tried to give Adi a high five but Adi completely missed it.

"Go sports," Adi said awkwardly. Then he turned back to Britt. "Well, I believe Mr. Henderson is still waiting for you" referring to the body on her prep table.

He grabbed an apple, took a bite and walked out the front door, heading to the doors to the funeral home. Britton was right behind him. "Seriously, what do you make of those guys on the news?"

"I have no idea, maybe they're ghosts," he said, making OOOoooOO ghost sounds.

"That's my fault for asking, but those were more than cheap Halloween costumes. From what I've seen at the Medizinhistorisches Museum in Switzerland and the Oddities Museum in Boston, they looked pretty authentic."

"Maybe they're stage quality, maybe bad advertising for a new play or something?" Adi suggested.

"Possibly, but Maine isn't really known for its live theatre. Maybe wing nut survivalists trying to create a panic?"

"I guess, we may never know. Now, shall we get to this?" Adi asked as he suggestively snapped on his rubber gloves. "After you Doctor," he said to Britt as he held the door to the morgue open for her.

"Look, Adi, I want to talk to you about something."

"Oh no, the talk. But we aren't even dating, this can't be good."

"Shut up," she responded playfully. "Seriously though, I'm going to try to figure out what this guy died of. If you're not comfortable with that, you can leave. No hard feelings."

"Well, those bad men from last night could come back at any time, but how else would I rather spend the rest of my life but as a prisoner in some dark cave somewhere. I'm in."

"You sure?" Britt asked.

"No, but I'll stay anyway. I could never resist a good mystery. How are you planning on doing this with no lab equipment?"

"I have no idea, but we have to do something. I'll start with collecting samples and see where we can go from there."

"Sounds good," Adi responded with a weird positive energy Britt hadn't really seen before. "I brought you these."

His eyes wide and bright like he was giving her a present and was way more excited about it than she was.

"What is it?" she asked.

"Go ahead. Open it," he said, almost giddy.

"Alrighty." She opened the box and saw a dozen hypodermic needles, a few Petri dishes, and some microscope slides. She closed the lid fast like she had just sneaked a peek into the Ark of the Covenant.

"What the? Where? How? Wait. What?" she said as she opened the box again. "Adi, how did you get this?"

"It was mine from when I was a child, my parents kept it up in their attic."

"You know what they'd do if they found this?"

"I do, that's why I wanted to get it out of their place," he said with a smile.

"Fair enough, but this is great. If only you still had the microscope."

"You mean this?" Adi replied, as he lifted a microscope out from behind the prep table and the body he was working.

"Adi, you never fail to surprise me. When did you bring all this here?"

"I went to my parent's place last night and got it from the attic. I figured you'd need it today. Then, I was too excited to sleep. I was here over an hour before you finally got up, lazy bones."

"Adi, I could just hug you right now."

"Awww," he said as he held his arms open for her embrace.

"Nah," they both said in unison, with a smile.

Britt was jarred awake by a series of loud knocks on her front door. She began to panic, thinking that it was the government coming back for another inspection. Her heart was racing as she put on her housecoat. She started to think about the tests; she couldn't remember if she had hidden them or if they were out in plain view. She became concerned that she would be one of the many medical professionals that had disappeared in the dark of the night, leaving Hunter to wonder what happened to her. She was almost in tears by the time she answered the door. To her shock, it was Adi. She yelled at him.

"What the fuck dude? What time is it? What are you doing here?"

He pushed his way past her, ignoring her questions, her messy hair and the little bit of drool in the corner of her mouth. Those things he would have normally made fun of, but not tonight.

"Have you seen the news?" he asked, almost as if he was in a panic.

"No, clearly not. I was in bed sleeping, like most reasonable people."

"Mom, what's going on?" Hunter asked from the shadows of the hallway.

"Nothing buddy, it's just Adi. Go back to bed. We'll talk in the morning."

"Okay, mom," he said. He walked part way down the hall and stopped to listen. She knew he was still there but didn't press the issue. By this time Adi had the TV on. The news had the same clip on repeat. It was a close up of several men dressed up like plague doctors walking into a hospital. They completely ignored the staff as they pushed their way down the hall. The camera followed, but not too closely. Two by two, they went into different patients' rooms. Then, just seconds later, they reappeared, dragging sick people out of the rooms and down the hallway. The staff again tried to stop them, but despite their best efforts, they couldn't even slow the costumed men down. A security guard came running up, he yelled at them to stop. He was pushed aside with ease as the 20 men dragged 10 patients out of the hospital. There was one remaining plague doctor trailing the pack. Several people tried to stop him. The man stopped, looked at the person with the camera, he grabbed the beak of his mask and said something that was barely audible to the camera. After the very brief exchange, the masked man left.

The group, including the camera operator, followed them out. When they stepped out of the hospital, they walked into a very eerie fog. The last plague doctor was barely visible, and then disappeared from sight completely. A couple of the braver hospital staff members ran into the fog after them, but as they got into the fog, it disappeared, along with the costumed men and the patients. The camera cut out as the staff members all looked on, scared and confused.

The news anchors started dissecting the incident. They were trying to make sense of the only word the group said. One newscaster said, "If you listen, it sounds like they're saying 'asthma' or 'my asthma'."

Adi's eyes were wide when he turned to Britt.

"What do you make of this?" he asked. "You okay?"

She was whiter than normal. She had goosebumps and the hairs on her arms were standing up.

"What's wrong?" Adi said again.

"It can't be," Britt said, still in a trance-like state.

"What is it?" Adi asked again.

Britt was flipping through books and opening up her thesis on her desk. "That word. They weren't saying 'asthma' or 'my asthma'. They were saying 'miasma'."

"Wait, they weren't saying 'my asthma', they were saying 'my asthma'?"

"No, not 'my….asthma'" she said accentuating the point with her hands. "Miasma. It's an old English word. It means 'bad air." It was what they thought caused the black plague in the 1300s. The word itself was essentially not used after they figured out the plague wasn't an airborne virus. No one uses it anymore."

"What does that mean?" Adi prompted.

"I have no friggin' idea," she said. "Wait. Where was this?"

"I think they said Trenton," Adi answered.

"New Jersey?" Britt said puzzled.

"Yes, New Jersey," he said sarcastically. "No, Trenton, Maine."

"Give me a break, I'm supposed to be asleep," she said playfully. "Do something useful. Get on a local news site and see if anything about flowers is mentioned."

"For here?"

"Yes, for here." It was her turn to be sarcastic. "No dumbass, in Trenton…Maine."

As he was looking up the information online, she was looking up more information about the plague.

"Odd," Adi said. "Yesterday a local woman in the town paper was complaining that vandals had destroyed her prize flower garden. Weird though, they didn't mention what kind of prize she won for her posies."

Britt gave him a 'seriously' glance at the extra information he provided. He simply shrugged and smiled.

"That can't be." She said over and over again.

"Britt, you can't seriously think they were 14th-century plague doctors."

"Of course not, but yes. Maybe?" She knew she was being crazy.

"It is probably some vigilante group trying to scare people. Or it's a group of modern doctors trying to treat people in secret, and they're using those costumes to be anonymous."

"Possibly, but where did they go when the fog lifted?"

"Hear me out. Maybe it was members of the hospital staff. They were all in on it, and with some quick editing they made it look like they disappeared."

"To what end?" Britt asked.

"I don't know. Maybe the government was closing in on them, so they went underground."

"Went underground. Look at you being all gangster," Britt teased.

Adi gave her a fake smile and continued. "Look, if you knew you could treat these people, like cure them instead of just feeding them until they die and hope they don't spread their diseases to others, what would you do?"

"I'd find a way to treat them."

"Exactly."

By morning there were several other reports of the same activity. Mysterious men that appeared and disappeared in a fog, dragging the sick with them. Britt felt confident with their conclusion from the night before. With the popularity of steampunk and the old plague masks being a staple of that art form, maybe they were using the costumes as commentary on the current situation. She started to wonder how she could get in touch with them to give them a hand.

Six months had passed since Adi had woken Britton up in the middle of the night and showed her the first clear incident of plague doctors caught on film. Since that time, the President had once again declared that this was not the time for an election. People were too sick, and resources too exhausted to do anything about it. During that time, the incidents of preventable diseases, like the measles, polio and chicken pox, had continued to rise. The previously-vaccinated and the naturally-immune had been called to duty, to help wherever they could.

Also on the rise were the reports of plague doctors and the disappearance of the sick. The incidents of patients being taken into the abyss of the mysterious fog was rising rapidly, with occurrences happening almost nightly. Although Britt never mentioned it, she was growing concerned for Hunter. She had no idea who the people were, or how they decided who they were going to take, but with Hunter living so close to a funeral home, and all the potential life threatening diseases that came and went on a daily basis, she was worried that it was only a matter of time before he, too, got sick.

Oddly, attacks by the public on places like hospitals and labs had increased because the angry mobs felt they weren't doing enough to help, despite it being a crime to actually do something. It was a no-win situation. Not for the men and women of medicine, and not for the public.

Random attacks had also been happening on Britt's funeral home. It started with graffiti, and escalated to smashing windows. Britt didn't understand it. Even if there was no law, she wasn't a medical doctor or even a lab. She just assumed it was locals trying to mimic what had been going on online, and since there were no labs or hospitals in Aurora, Maine, she was the next best thing.

The fact that she wasn't a lab or a hospital was abundantly clear to her. She and Adi weren't able to do any real analysis of the samples they collected. Not only did they not have the proper equipment, but when it came to diseases and viruses, the biggest obstacle to overcome was that they needed a live host, as the samples died shortly after the host did. That didn't stop either of them from trying to come up with solutions though.

Finally, Britt made the decision that she was going to go to the CDC to see what they could do, or to see if they could confirm that the black plague was, in fact, alive and well in the USA. She figured going to visit them may yield a better result than merely phoning them. The last person she had talked to didn't really seem that comfortable with talking on the phone. She asked Adi to stay with Hunter, but he insisted he travel with her, so she left Hunter with her aunt who lived on the way to Atlanta. Britt didn't really feel comfortable taking him to her aunt's. The more he was out, and the closer they got to a city, the higher the risk of him getting sick became. She knew she had to risk it, for him and possibly for the country.

When they got to the CDC, Britt was surprised at how empty the place was. She started to grow concerned that it may have been completely abandoned. They wandered down hallway after hallway looking for people, but found no one. They were beginning to wish they had brought their respirators with them. After all, just by the nature of the building, they knew some of the most deadly diseases on the planet were alive behind the doors they were walking past.

Finally, they went down a darkened hallway and pushed their way through a couple of swinging doors.

They were surprised to find a heavy set man, roughly in his mid-30s, eating pizza, watching Netflix and playing video games. His feet were up on the desk and he almost fell over when they walked through the door. Britt was amused at his surprise, and although they didn't say it, they were both relatively relieved that the man wasn't wearing a respirator either.

He got up to his feet, spilling Mountain Dew all over his shirt. "Damn, doesn't anyone knock anymore?"

Britt recognized his voice immediately. "You're James."

"At your service," he said, as he wiped his greasy hands off on his t-shirt. "And you are?"

"My name is Britt, I called you a few..."

"Oh yes, the plague lady."

Britt was amazed he remembered her.

"What can I do for you?" His question sounded sincere, but he was looking around like he was a rat stealing crack from a cat.

"You okay?" Adi asked.

"Ya, man. Why do you ask?"

"You just look, you look like you're expecting the boogeyman or something."

"No no, just can't be too careful these days. You know, with the new laws, those sons of bitches would do anything to throw us all in jail. Or worse."

Both Britt and Adi wished it was unfounded paranoia, but they were both worried enough working at a funeral home. They assumed that would be a million times worse at the CDC.

Britt refocused the group. "We were wondering if you had any word on the resurgence of the plague?"

"No, not that we can say, but well, who knows. We aren't allowed to go out and test anyone, and even if we did, there is nothing we could do about it. What did you find out from the body you called us about?"

"It was inconclusive. We just don't have the knowledge to make an accurate diagnosis. Could you test samples if you did have some?"

James leaned in close to Britt and started talking very clearly like he was presenting testimony to a court. "No. We here at the CDC cannot and will not test any unlawful samples, and we do not have the resources to do so, even if we wanted to."

"What the hell, man?" Britt asked.

"Oh, I believe this man believes you're wired," Adi suggested.

"Wired? What the hell dude?" She reached over and grabbed James by the shirt and pulled him in close. "We think the plague is back and it has something to do with those clowns dressing up as plague doctors, and we need to find out for sure."

"Okay, okay, calm down there. As I said, we really don't have the ability to test anything. I'm not sure what we can do to help. Besides, we would need a viable sample, and you said you worked at a funeral home, right? We can't test samples from the deceased."

"Ya, we figured that out. What if we had samples from a real live living person? I mean, a very very sick person, but still alive, nevertheless."

"Impossible. If you took samples from a living person 'they' would have known and we wouldn't be having this conversation. You'd be wherever scientists go when they break the rules."

"It was easy actually," Adi said. "We went to the hospital to pick up a body. Britt distracted the hospital staff and the guard, while I found a room with a woman in it that looked like she had the same plague symptoms we saw on the bodies. I got her blood, and samples of the purulent discharge, just to be sure."

Adi held up a paper bag that contained the samples, and he had a cheesy grin like he just stole the crown jewels.

"Put that down!" James yelled, as he grabbed at Adi's arm. "You want to get us all killed? Okay you two, come with me before you do get us killed."

James looked around, shifty like a detective in a 1950s movie.

Adi and Britt looked at each other and shrugged.

"Alright, an adventure. I don't know about Britt, but I'm definitely in for following this strange fellow further into this very creepy building."

Britt smiled and hit him on the shoulder.

The three walked through various labs and arrived in a relatively empty room. James stopped and looked around again, then stared at Adi and Britt. He looked them up and down for several minutes. "I'm taking a big risk doing this, don't fuck it up."

Neither of them understood, they just nodded in agreement. James walked over to a cabinet covered in dusty old lab equipment. He grabbed an old chemistry book and the cabinet made a clicking sound. Adi and Britt looked at each other quizzically. James pulled on a corner and it opened a door into a pristine room with three scientists working diligently. They all stopped dead in their tracks when they saw the foreign faces. James reassured them and apprised them of the situation. Adi gave them the sample and told them what they suspected. The lab workers put the sample in a nearby fridge. Adi and Britt just stood there. One of the scientists looked at them.

"What?"

"Oh, I'm sorry, I thought you were going to test that," Adi said.

"We will, but right now we have other diseases to sample, vaccines to make on a small scale that we can duplicate on a large scale once this nonsense is over, if it ever is, and now you're asking us to test something that can be cured with a simple antibiotic? We can't just stop when every Tom, Dick and..."

"Actually it's Britt and Adi," Adi interrupted. Everyone in the room stopped and looked at him. "Never mind, it's not important. You were saying?"

"I was saying, we'll get to it. When we figure out what it is, James will call you and say 'Pizza is ready' if it's the plague or 'sorry, our vacation has been canceled' if it's negative."

"Oh fun! Code. It's like we're spies. We're spies Britt," Adi said. Again, his attempt at humour fell flat, to everyone but him. He cleared his throat and took on a more authoritative voice. "Okay, if it is, when will you guys be able to distribute the antibiotics?"

"Oh, that won't be us. That will be entirely up to you."

"Us? We're Morticians, not scientists."

"I don't know what to tell you, we don't have the time or resources. Ok, look, I could get in major trouble for this, but here."

He handed them a manual, that looked like a CDC version of "vaccines for dummies." In it was all they needed to know about identifying diseases and curing them. There was even a chapter on basic antibiotics.

"The plague hasn't been a thing for 700 years. We know a little about it, but never really had to come up with a specific antibiotic for it because it doesn't affect many people anymore. We know it is spread through ticks and fleas and some small communities in Africa have been treating it with antibiotics with some success but there really needs to be a formula specific to the plague for it to be 100% effective. It should be rather easy to come up with something."

"Ya for scientists, not morticians," Britt said under her breath.

"I'm sorry, we just can't help you with this undertaking."

"Oh, clever," Adi said with minimal enthusiasm.

"Look, I'm sorry we have too much to do, we can't just drop everything. This isn't the 1300s, stopping the spread of the plague and coming up with a cure will be easy. Just follow the manual."

Neither Britt nor Adi were comfortable with that answer, but it was painfully obvious that was as far as they were going to get, which was further ahead than they had been earlier that day. They thanked them for their time and left the secret lab. As he accompanied them back to his station, James cautioned them about speaking about what they saw. They both promised to take the secret to their grave, which they worried may be sooner rather than later.

"Oh, one last thing," he said, as they said goodbye. "Do not google anything. If 'they' hit on a keyword or two, game over, you two will be done."

They looked back, thanked him for the warning, and walked out the door.

On the way back, Adi read the book while Britt drove. "Oh, this should be easy. We just need to reinvent the wheel. Without rubber, wood, steel or aluminum, and no experience making wheels."

"Comforting," Britt replied.

Britton picked up Hunter, and on the way home, he started coughing. Adi and Britt looked at each other.

"You okay buddy?" Britt asked.

"Ya mom, I think I'm getting a cold. My throat hurts."

Both Adi and Britt knew a cold could mean much more in this day and age. "Okay, we'll keep an eye on it. What did you do at Aunt Kim's?"

"Just played video games. Oh, and she got this new kitten. She said she found it outside last week without a mommy, so she kept it."

Britt looked back at Hunter in the rearview mirror. Adi knew better than to say something, but she could see the same concern on his face.

They turned on the radio to break the silence. The announcer was talking about how the hospitals and funeral homes couldn't keep up with all the many dead bodies. People had begun burning the dead in open fields, and in some cities they had even begun to burn down funeral homes and hospitals in an effort to kill the diseases. That was all they heard before Britt turned off the radio and looked back again at Hunter. She didn't want to show fear for him or her business.

Hunter's health continued to deteriorate. Britt was in denial, but Adi knew their time was running out. He was doing his best to come up with a cure, but his knowledge and skills were limited. Luckily for them all, he was exceedingly smart, and loved a challenge. Britt wasn't sure when he went home to sleep, because he seemed to be in the morgue 24 hours a day working.

Britt knew she should have been down in the morgue with him, but she had to be upstairs, to be with Hunter, and to try and keep the vandals at bay. It was against every fiber of her being to hold a gun, but she broke out the shotgun her dad had kept in a safe in the garage with his old hearse. She told herself it was to scare vandals and possible arsonists, but deep down she knew it was to stop any of those costume vigilantes from taking her son into the fog with them.

Two weeks after they came back from their trip to the CDC, Adi came upstairs, he had a look of defeat on his face. Britt knew whatever he was about to say wasn't going to be good news. "I'm so sorry, I'm trying. The book is good, but I just don't have the materials or expertise. We need help. We need to go back to the CDC."

Holding back tears for fear of making Adi feel guilty, Britt said, "Okay, we'll call them in the morning."

She knew they weren't going to call them. She knew they couldn't help. She felt like she really was on her own. Giving up on Hunter wasn't an option. When Adi left to get a few hours' sleep at home, she agonized about what could be done to help her son. Their only real option was to find the underground science network James had mentioned. It would be dangerous, but what else could she do?

A few hours later she heard some noise in front of the house. She grabbed the gun and went to investigate. First, she looked out the window and saw nothing. There didn't appear to be any movement in the shadows, but she knew if people were out to cause harm, they wouldn't just stroll around in plain sight. She put on her housecoat and ran down the stairs and to the front door. She had no idea what she would do if she found anyone, but the gun was comforting in this dire situation. She even considered yelling like a mad woman and firing off a warning shot. It would definitely be a spur of the moment decision.

She flung open the door and ran outside, ready for combat. What she saw was soul crushing. She stopped dead and dropped the gun to her side. Her eyes filled with tears and she was too paralyzed to move. The noise she had heard had been someone picking the flowers in the beds on either side of her steps. She desperately hoped it could be a coincidence, a prank, but she knew deep down it wasn't. They were coming for her son. She wanted to call Adi, but there was nothing he could do, and she didn't want to put him at risk. She didn't know how they would react when seriously threatened, but she knew she would do anything to keep her son with her.

The next few hours were hell. She waited at the top of the steps while Hunter slept. She didn't move, not to pee, not to get a drink, and barely enough to blink. It was dawn when she noticed an eerie fog roll in, surrounding her place. Through the windows, she could only see a dark grey. The house got cold and the hairs on her arms began to stand up. Her fingers clenched the gun tightly as she very slowly descended the stairs. As she reached the bottom step, the door was flung open. Three plague doctors walked right in. She stepped in front of them, holding the gun up. They didn't even flinch, they just walked by like she wasn't even there. She began crying and yelling at them with a shrill panicked voice, but they still didn't acknowledge her.

She heard her son scream for her. She went to run up the stairs after them, but one of the doctors was at the bottom of the stairs with his back to her. Nothing she could do would make him move or even look at her. She wanted to shoot him in the back, but as she raised the barrel she couldn't pull the trigger. She wanted too, she wanted to protect Hunter but taking someone's life was just something she couldn't bring herself to do. What if it did turn out that they were there to help? But if they were, why didn't they just tell her? The questions danced around in her head as she watched as the events transpire.

She dropped her arms, still holding the gun to her side. She saw one doctor carrying her son, with another behind him. Hunter was crying and screaming for his mom, but the doctor's grip was just too secure for him to be able to wiggle loose. The doctor at the bottom of the stairs turned around and moved out of their way, blocking Britt from getting to her son. As the others walked by, the doctor that had stayed with her turned and looked at her. Once again she raised the barrel of the shotgun, pointing it at him, though her hands were shaking, and tears were running down her face.

The doctor reached up, pushed the barrel away, and leaned into her. He was face to face with her, but she couldn't see into the lenses of the mask to see who the person may have been. Barely audible, he leaned even closer and said "miasma" as he touched the beak of his mask.

She dropped the gun to the ground as they walked through the door. It closed behind them, and she gathered herself and ran after them. As she flung the door open, the last doctor was disappearing into the fog, and within seconds, they were gone with her son. She fell to the ground crying.

Not being one to give in to emotions, she soon pulled herself together and got up. Her hands were still shaking and tears were still flowing, but she went into action. She was just about to call Adi when her phone rang.

"Hello?"

"Your pizza is ready. It's a specialty order, the original recipe just won't work."

She had known for a while that it was the plague, but the confirmation was still enough to shake her. She had no idea what the rest meant. Maybe it was just their attempt to throw off anyone listening. Before she could ask any questions the line went dead. She was frustrated but knew they had to be safe.

Adi walked in the front door. Britt was focused now, the time for tears was over, and it was time for action.

"They have Hunter," she told Adi, matter-of-factly.

"What? Who has Hunter?"

"Them, they, the doctors. They took him 10 minutes ago. We have to do something."

"Crikey," he said. Normally Britt would mock him for using a word like crikey, but she wasn't in the mood for their normally playful banter. She grabbed her coat and put it on.

"Britt, what are you doing? Where are you going?" he asked.

"CDC, they just called. It is the plague but they said something about the standard recipe won't work, that it's a specialty order. We have to find out what they mean and make them find the cure so I can go get Hunter."

"A specialty order? That is odd. Just give me time to think, collect my notes and we need to come up with a plan. We won't do anyone any good if we go off half-cocked and end up in a government holding cell."

Britt reluctantly agreed. He also forced her to eat and tried to get her to sleep while he was working. She did lie down, but sleep wasn't in her immediate future. Finally, when Adi had everything he thought he was going to need, he went to Britt's room and they called the CDC.

"Hello, James speaking."

They both noticed he didn't say CDC like last time, but thought it was just an innocent mistake.

"It's Britt and Adi, we have an emergency."

"Look. Like I told you last time we talked, we can't do anything for you."

"They took my son," Britt screamed.

"I'm sorry, we just can't…"

They heard a loud bang in the background, followed by a lot of yelling. They heard the sound of the phone hitting the ground, and then the sound of a man getting the wind knocked out of him. They heard faint breathing.

"What's going on?" they asked.

James' voice said, "Paul Harris."

And then the phone went dead.

"Who's Paul Harris?" they asked into the phone. "Hello?"

There was no response. The stress was starting to show on Britt's face. Adi knew he needed to step up, and step up fast. He made a pot of coffee as they pondered what the importance of the "Paul Harris". As the pot was brewing, Adi googled the name.

"It says here he was the last director of the CDC before…well, before," he said.

"What? So, why would he mention his name? Do you think if we find him, he can help us?"

"Maybe. Oh, nope. It says here he was one of the first people to disappear under the new policies."

Adi poured them both a coffee and they sat in silence as their minds raced. Adi was the first to break the silence. "Wait, what if…never mind it's probably nothing."

"What is it?" she prompted. "We might be able to work with nothing, nothing is all we have right now."

"Well, what if the answer is in his office at the CDC?" Adi asked.

"What if it's not? Or, if it is, how do we know they didn't empty out the entire building or burn it to the ground?" Britt questioned.

"We don't, but what else do we have?"

"They could be there waiting for us. Maybe I'd better go by myself," she suggested. She didn't like the idea of putting her friend further at risk.

"If there are answers, you're going to need me. If there aren't any answers, you're still going to need me," he said stated. They slipped into silence again.

"I just had a frightening thought!" he blurted out.

"Not another one, what was it?" she asked hesitantly.

"Well, those guys that got James, and I assume his friends, will most likely be checking to see who called them. It won't be long before they come for us."

"Yup," she said. She had a look of panic, fright, anger, and frustration. She ran upstairs and threw some clothes in a bag, and they went to look for a car they could use. They knew they couldn't use their cars and if they stole one, the cops would soon be looking for it. They didn't have to look far, though. Britt suggested they take her dad's classic hearse, it had been the company's very first hearse. It was old and didn't have plates on it. Since it hadn't been registered in a very long time, she was hoping the government wouldn't think to look for it.

Luckily, after a quick boost, the old car started right up. Stopping at the neighbours, they borrowed plates from a car Britt knew they rarely used. They were hoping they'd be out of state before anyone noticed the plates or the old hearse was missing.

"Not exactly subtle," Adi said, as they got back into the car.

"Hopefully being so conspicuous will work in our favour," Britt said.

"Possibly."

"Oh, we'll need to make a stop in Boston before we go too far," Britt added as she put the car in drive and hit the accelerator.

"I don't think this is the time for sightseeing, Britt."

"Trust me."

As Britt drove the old Cadillac hearse down the highway, Adi kept his head in the books trying to solve their problem. Adi knew that learning how to make a cure was going to be just the tip of the iceberg. After that, they'll need to find the ingredients, mix them properly and then make them on a mass scale. He had no idea how to do any of that, so he kept reading, hoping for a miracle.

He was so focused on his books, he didn't realize Britt had parked the car. He looked up, at her and then at his surroundings.

"Oh no Britt, what are you doing here?" he said as he stared at the Museum of Oddities in Boston. "Britt, I have to object. You can't be doing what I think you're doing."

"Hold on," she told him in an authoritative voice he hadn't heard from her before. She walked up to the door, which, much to Adi's relief, was locked, which wasn't surprising considering it was 3 a.m.

"Can we just get going? There has to be a better way."

He had barely finished the sentence, when she picked up a rock and threw it through a window. She disappeared into the black of the museum, while the alarm pierced the quiet streets. In just a few minutes, she had the back door of the old car open and she tossed something in. Adi didn't even have to look to know she had stolen the authentic plague suit. He didn't ask her any questions, or what she was going to use it for, but he knew it wasn't going to be good.

She jumped in the driver's seat and took off with the urgency of a getaway driver leaving the scene of a crime, because that's exactly what she was. Adi just mumbled under his breath while shaking his head. He couldn't believe, with everything that was going on, he was now an accomplice to a break and enter. Britt could tell he was under great stress. He was a good man and wouldn't even consider jaywalking, let alone helping her steal the suit. She felt guilty, but she knew breaking into the Museum wouldn't be the worst thing they would be doing over the next few days.

Trying to comfort him, she said, "Relax dude, I'll bring it back, I pinky swear."

She held up her pinky finger.

Britt always put on a tough exterior like nothing ever got to her, and even though she was trying to be light and calm for Adi, he knew she was anything but. Even though her sarcasm and humour, he knew she would do absolutely anything to get her son back, and his disappearance was eating her alive.

As she drove the car through the quiet city streets she noticed a bright neon sign flashing the word 'open.' She slowed the car as she drove by.

"No friggin' way."

"What?" Adi asked as he looked up from his textbook. "You can't be serious, they probably just left the sign on, it's 3 in the morning, there is no way they're open."

"You're probably right," she said, as she stopped the car and put it in park.

"I don't like this Britt, need I remind you that we just committed a break and enter? We shouldn't be sightseeing."

"You can wait in the car if you want- I just remember reading posts on some blogs from the owner of this store. He kept talking about ghost plague doctors appearing all over the world. They take the sick and disappear into the fog. At the time I thought he was crazy, and completely forgot about him until just now."

"Okay, even if he's for real, there is no chance he is actually open. Unless you think it's some kind of omen," Adi said sarcastically.

"Maybe it is," she said as she pulled open the door to Ya Sang's Occult and Paranormal Paraphernalia. They were greeted by a white man in his late 50's who was sitting behind the counter reading a paper.

"Good morning, what can I do for you?" the shop owner asked.

"We're surprised to see you here...open I mean," Adi said.

"I've been expecting you," the shopkeeper said in a sinister tone.

"Creepy," Adi whispered to Britt.

"I'm just messing with you, I live above the shop and suffer from insomnia. Nights I can't sleep, I'll come down here and open up. You'd be surprised by the amount of people who come looking around in the middle of the night. I'm Ray, I'm the owner. What brings you in tonight?"

"Hi Ray, I'm Britt and this is Adi. We have a couple of questions we hope you can answer."

"I'll do my best."

Adi jumped in before Britt could get her questions out. "So, did you buy this place from a guy named Ya Sang?"

With a chuckle Ray replied. "No, Ya Sang is a form of black magic performed in Thailand. I spent some time there in the 80s and what I learnt there sparked my interest in the occult and paranormal. I thought it was a fitting tribute. And besides, it sounds more authentic than Ray's Occult shop or something silly like that."

"Fair enough," Adi replied.

Britt jumped in before either of them could start talking again. "What do you know about these plague doctors? I saw a post of yours a few years ago and you talked about them being ghosts?"

"Oh yes, the plague doctors. Well, I gotta tell ya, it has been an interesting few months for sure. All I have is theories and no proof."

"They have my son, a good theory is a lot better than what we have now."

"I'm sorry to hear that, but if they are who I think they are, they are trying their best to help him."

"Who do you think they are?" Adi asked.

"Well, I've heard stories that they were summoned through a practice called Goetia, mostly because the earliest records we have of the appearance of these paranormal plague doctors was in a 17th-century grimoire called the Lesser Key of Solomon. The story suggests that King Solomon was dealing with an increased level of sick subjects, so he used Goetia as a form of good magic or a charm to combat the evil magic that had a grip on his subjects…"

"But you don't believe that?" Britt asked, hanging off his every word.

"No, what I believe is these doctors are spirits stuck in what the Catholics would call purgatory. They are doctors that died during the plague but don't know they're dead so they keep showing up to do the job they were given in life."

"Oh ya, that's way more believable." Adi said sarcastically.

Ignoring Adi, Ray continued. "They don't mean to do anyone harm. The problem is, they are still using the technology and science they had back then and that in itself can be deadly."

"What can we do to get my son and the others back?"

"I'm sorry, that I can't answer. There have been some reports of people being returned once they got better but those that returned are considerably fewer than those taken. Sadly, for the most part once they're gone, they stay gone."

"But, if we get the sick treatment, they'll be returned right?" Britt asked anxiously.

"Possibly, look, this is all just a theory. Even if that were true, how would you get them the antibiotics they need?"

"I may have a plan," Britt said, thinking about her plague suit, but she didn't elaborate. "Do you know what they're trying to say? Do you know anything about their language? All I could understand was 'miasma', but the rest sounds like gibberish."

"Again, there are several theories. The two prevailing theories are they are speaking Enochian..."

"Enochian? I don't think I've heard of that," Adi said.

"Enochian is an Angelic language, first mentioned by John Dee, a Philosopher and advisor to Queen Elizabeth the first. He claimed the language was revealed to him by Enochian angels. I don't buy that though. My theory is, if they are doctors that were alive during the first plague pandemic, they are most likely speaking Anglo-Saxon English, the foundation of the English we speak today. Authors such as William Shakespeare played an integral part in bridging the gap between our language and that of the Anglo-Saxons."

"So, if it's a form of English, we should be able to communicate with them right?" Britt asked.

"Not really. English has adapted from many other languages like Latin and Greek, Anglo-Saxons had more of a Celtic influence. You would have a better chance of having a conversation in Italian than you would in Anglo-Saxon."

"Does anyone speak the language now? Is there an English to English translation book?" Britt asked.

"There are a handful of people in the world that still use the old English, but there is only one that I know of that speaks Anglo-Saxon English and our English, and he lives in rural Ireland. I don't have a book that translates words directly, like you would if you were travelling to Paris and wanted to speak in French, but I do have a sort of dictionary that explains the meaning of many old English words. It was created by Shakespeare himself, but has since been added to by many authors throughout the years. I'll go grab it."

Ray got off his stool and went behind a beaded curtain into a back room.

Whispering, Adi leaned into Britt. "You can't believe any of this, can you?"

"It's all we have, besides, how else can you explain any of this?"

"I don't know, but ghosts? Purgatory? It is just too much."

"All of this is too much. I'd rather believe they are doctors trying to cure Hunter and will give him back once he's well, than assume he's gone forever and we can't do anything to bring him back."

"You're right, I'm sorry Britt. We can work with this new information. Hopefully I can work on making antibiotics and you can work on learning the dead language. All we need to figure out now is how do we use this new information to get to Hunter?"

"I have a plan, I'll explain it if we get that far."

"Right, the plague suit," Adi said hesitantly.

Ray returned with an old book and showed it to the pair. "This is it, it's not an easy read but it's all I have."

"Thank you," Britt said as she started thumbing through the pages. "It reads like a Shakespeare play."

"Well, I did tell you he had a huge part in writing it."

"Right. How much do we owe you for it?"

"I'm sorry, this is part of my private collection, so it's not for sale."

"Ok, I understand, is there a version online or can we photocopy some of the pages?" Britt asked, with an air of desperation.

"Look, you seem like good people. I'll tell you what. I'll loan you that book, but when you do whatever it is you're planning on doing, you tell me about your experience on my podcast. Deal?"

"Deal," Britt said, extending her hand.

"Excellent," Ray said. He handed them a card. "Call me if you need anything else."

"Will do Ray, thank you so much for your help," Britt said as they left the store.

Once they got outside, Adi turned to her. "I wish that was the weirdest thing I've done this week."

"It's just the tip of the iceberg," Britt said with a renewed sense of optimism.

"Great," Adi replied hesitantly.

They returned to their car and set off for Atlanta. The rest of the car trip was quiet as Adi researched and Britt kept an eye out for potential government agents.

After several long hours, they finally made it to Atlanta. In an effort at caution, they tried to recall every spy movie they could think of to outthink the feds. They parked several blocks away, leaving the hearse deep in a parking garage. They knew a hearse was going to get some attention, but hopefully not from the wrong people. They caught themselves tiptoeing up the sidewalk, then they laughed at themselves, knowing their attempt at being inconspicuous was going to make them stand out. They stood up straight, and walked with confidence toward the building.

They 'staked the place out' for a few minutes to see if there was any movement. Everything was eerily silent, but they knew they couldn't waste any more time, so they slowly approached the building. She pulled on the door and it opened. They weren't sure if that was a good sign or bad, but either way, they proceeded with extreme caution.

Adi had many wonderful traits, and his near perfect memory was one of them. He managed to navigate them to the room where they had first met James. Still being very cautious, they slowly opened the door.

James wasn't there. The room had been destroyed, and there was a pool of congealed blood on the floor.

Being careful not to step in any of it, they made their way to the secret door and they both took a deep breath as he opened it. They were both horrified to see the room had been discovered. All the research was gone, there was more blood on the floor, and all the equipment had either been destroyed or removed. Their hearts sank.

"What now?" Britt asked with a pitch in her voice that sounded like she was about to have a total and complete breakdown. Adi too felt the sting of defeat but knew he needed to be strong for her.

"It's okay Britt, let's go find Paul Harris's office."

"How? This place is huge."

"The higher in the building, the more important the people are, right?"

"I didn't know that was a thing," she said, trying to regain some composure.

"Oh, sure it is. You never see a CEO on the first floor do you?"

"I guess you're right," she agreed. "Let's go up then."

They made their way through the maze and up the stairs. The upper levels had not been used in years, by the look of it. Desks were covered in cobwebs, and dust lay thickly on the ground.

They finally saw the name Paul Harris on a big wooden door. Adi put his hand on the door.

"Here goes nothing."

He turned the knob and pushed. The door opened to reveal a big, empty room. Not a bookcase, no desk, nothing. They still looked around, hoping to find a trap door or secret room, but there was nothing.

"What are we going to do now?" Britt said as she began to cry. "This can't be it. Hunter is all I have left. We can't just give up."

Adi gave her a hug.

"This is a big building Britt. We will search one office at a time if we have to, until we find something. There has to be equipment or a clue around here somewhere."

They started to go from office to office on the top floor, finding one empty room after another. As they were walking down one hall, they saw pictures of all the past directors, a long line of older white men.

"They're all about diversity here," Britt joked.

Another trait Adi possessed was his keen eye for detail. He stopped, reached out and grabbed Britt by the back of her shirt and pulled her towards him.

"What are you doing, dude?"

"Look," he said, nodding in the direction of one of the pictures.

"Ya, an old white guy. I noticed."

"No. Look," he pointed at the picture.

"What? It looks like all the others."

"No, it doesn't. This one is pushed out slightly further than the others, and it's not level."

"It was probably just hit when they were taking the furniture away," she said. "Come on, we don't have time to admire art, we need to find something that can help us."

"Just a second. Look at the name."

The picture was of none other than director Paul Harris.

"Do you think?" he asked as he pulled the picture off the wall. He looked at Britt hopefully and then turned the picture around and found nothing. Again, their hopes were crushed. They knew it was a long shot, and that things like a hidden map or clue on the back of a picture was only something that happened in the movies. Adi went to hang the picture up, but it slipped from the hook and fell to the ground, breaking the frame.

A broken frame hardly seemed to matter now. They began to walk down the hallway. Adi did have slight OCD, so he only made it about 5 steps before he had to run back and try to hang it the best he could. When he picked it up, the frame fell completely apart.

"I'd have thought someplace like the CDC would have better quality frames," Britt joked.

Adi agreed, and then curiosity got the better of him. He began breaking the frame into pieces. Then he grabbed the picture and held it up to the light. Again, nothing. They both knew at that point they had watched way too many movies. Britt slammed her back against the wall, her head hitting the wall harder than she intended before she slid down to the floor.

"What are we doing here? This is a dead end."

She picked up a piece of the frame and threw it against the wall and buried her head in her hands.

"Britt," Adi said. She ignored him.

"Britt, look at this."

"What is it?" she asked, tired and defeated.

He didn't respond, but just started picking at the wall above her, where the portrait had been. The dust started falling on her.

"What the hell dude."

She scrambled to her feet. When her head had hit the wall, it had cracked open a brick that was behind the picture. Adi kept digging behind the false brick. He found a cubby hole that contained a key and a hand-drawn map. It looked like it had been there for years.

"What does it say?" Britt asked.

"'If you're reading this, the war on science is almost over. We are losing, and the CDC has fallen. If there is anyone left, you know where to find them.' I'm assuming this was meant for someone else," Adi said.

"Let me see it," Britt said. "There has to be more, where can we find them?"

"I have no idea," Adi added as he continued to dig in the cubby hole. He found another tube with a note in it. When he opened it, it just had the common names of different elements.

"Odd for a bunch of world-class scientists," said Britt.

The elements listed were: Lanthanum, Boron, Nickel written upside down, Boron, Actinium, Potassium, Nobelium, Dubnium.

They looked at the note for a long time, trying to understand the meaning to it. They hoped they were smart enough to figure it out. They both were very familiar with the periodic table of elements through their studies, but they didn't know what this meant.

"Is it a recipe?" Britt wondered aloud.

She started writing down the elements using their symbols. For Lanthanum, she wrote La, B for boron and so on, until she had La, B, Ni, B, Ac, K, No, Db. They both stared at the names and symbols.

"La could stand for Los Angeles or Louisiana," Adi suggested.

"If we have to go to LA, we're screwed," Britt said with fear in her voice.

"We need to do this," she said, encouraging herself and him to keep going. "What numbers are associated with the elements?"

Adi wrote them out: 57, 5, 28, with 82 in brackets in case upside down meant inversed, 5, 89, 19, 102 and finally 105. They both racked their brains trying to come up with a mathematical solution, a scientific solution and a combination of both.

"This is so frustrating! What does it mean?" Britt almost yelled.

"I have no idea," he answered, and both felt as far away from a solution as they had been before they arrived in Atlanta.

After starting at it until they felt cross-eyed, Britt said, "No fucking way. It can't be this obvious, could it?"

She started rewriting the symbols without commas. La B Ni B Ac K No Db. "It said Lab Ni Back No Db."

"No, wait," Adi interrupted as he turned the Ni upside down. "Lab in back no db. No Db? What does that mean? Decibels? No decibels? Do they have a soundproof room here?"

"Lab in back of no 105?" she asked. Could it be a simple room number?

"If it was in, why not just use Indium instead of upside-down Nickel?" Adi asked.

"I have no idea. Maybe they wanted to make it a little challenging?"

"Alright, good enough for me. Let's find room 105."

They collected their notes, the clues and went to find 105.

After wandering around the huge facility for another 30 minutes, they finally found what they thought was room 105. The room number had been removed and others nearby seemed to have been changed, but they were confident it was the right room.

They opened the door and found a storage room. It was small, and definitely not a lab. There was something scratched into the wall at the back of the small room. The marks read XLIX. They both recognized it as the Roman numeral for 49.

"49?" she said, and at the same time, they both said, "Indium."

"Lets go 'In'," joked Ali

They stepped fully into the room, but nothing happened. They decided to close the door to see if that would help. When they did, the room went pitch black, except for a light switch that started glowing a bright green once the door closed. Without hesitation, Britt flicked it on.

Nothing happened. She flicked it off and on again and a black light sparked to life. It revealed an arrow pointing to the ground, and a small circle that said: "push here."

Adi said, "Let me get this one."

He dropped to his knees and pushed the spot on the wall. It was a large doggy door. The room was so small, they really couldn't look in without physically going through the door.

"Here goes nothing," he said as he crawled through the door.

Britt was close behind him. The room on the other side was pitch black. They both started feeling the walls until Britt felt what she thought was a light switch. She turned it on and a fluorescent light flickered on. She quickly turned on the other three switches.

The lights revealed a large lab. The storage room was a cheap plywood built around the only entrance. Whoever had built the false front had definitely been expecting trouble. The room was full of equipment, dusty but functional. It also had a full library and a computer system. They talked about turning the computer on, but decided against it in case it could be traced.

"This should do the trick," Adi said, trying to restrain his excitement because he knew they still faced an uphill battle. As he reminded himself, he was not actually a scientist.

They knew they had to get to work fast if they were going to find a cure. Britt didn't think about the next move. Even if they made a cure, how would they get it to Hunter?

Knowing time was of the essence, they got to work. Britt scoured the library while Adi took inventory of the supplies. Thanks to his research on the trip to Atlanta, he had a good idea of what he would need, he just had no idea what to do once he got the materials together.

Britt started with the obvious: books on the plague, black plague, Black Death and 14th-century diseases. The problem she encountered was that it was a science library, not a public library. Books and reference materials weren't organized or even named in the conventions she was used to. She once again began to feel like it was a lost cause, but she paused, thought about Hunter, took a deep breath and got back to work. She heard the crashing of a large amount of glass breaking. She looked over at Adi.

"My bad," was all he said with a guilty smile.

She smiled and went back to work. She had no idea where she'd be without him. Not only did he have a brilliant mind, but he also made life look effortless, and approached everything with a light-hearted attitude. More often than not, this attitude kept her grounded and focused. She didn't know it, but the reason he stayed with her as her assistant, despite many job offers elsewhere, was the same level of respect he felt for her. He felt he had much to learn from her, and her dedication and work ethic was second to none. They were a perfect pair.

Britt finally found the book they were looking for, and together they gathered all the appropriate materials. The entire process took much longer than either of them wanted. Led by Adi, they made mixture after mixture. Some began to smoke and melt the glass, others didn't have the right colour, or reacted contrary to how the book said it would. The other problem they didn't discuss was, even if they made something they thought would work, they would have no way to test it. Not on animals and definitely not on people. Using Hunter as the guinea pig, if they could even get to him, wasn't ideal but may be the only option they had.

They were so focused on their work, they completely forgot where they were and what the outside world was like.

That changed fast when they heard the door of the broom closet slam shut and the false walls shake. They worried they were going to be caught and that would be the end of it. Britt ran to the light switch and killed the lights, as Adi found them a place to hide. Britt heard voices yelling in the hallway and what sounded like a person crying in the closet. The voices faded but the crying did not. Britt got on her hands and knees and was about to open the doggie door, but Adi told her to stop.

She whispered, “Don’t be so pusillanimous.”

“Really? Pusillanimous? Very nice,” he replied sarcastically in a loud whisper. “What if this person is one of ‘them’?”

“Think about it,” she answered, “If they thought we were in here or that there was even a lab in here, why play games? Why not just smash their way in, destroy the lab and haul us off to jail or wherever? Like they did with James and company.”

She ever so slowly opened the doggie door. She saw a man sitting down, holding his knees with tears running down his face. Taking a huge risk, she said hello. He jumped.

“Who are you?” the man in the closet asked.

“It’s okay, we’re not with them.” she said in an attempt to reassure him.

“How do I know you’re not with them?”

“If we were, we’d be screaming at the top of our lungs for the guys that chased you in here, right? Now get in here before they come back.”

He nodded in agreement and crawled through the small door.

"Oh my god," he said in amazement. "I'd heard rumours the CDC was still operating in secret. I'm so happy to have found you. How long have you been working here?"

Britt and Adi looked at each other awkwardly and Adi responded. "Well. About what, 6 hours? Give or take? We're...we aren't exactly scientists."

"No? What are you then?" the man asked with concern in his voice.

"Well, we're um...funeral directors."

"What? What are you doing here then?" he asked, as he looked over the materials they had gathered. "It looks like you're trying to make, what, antibiotics? For what?"

"The plague," Britt answered and went into the story of what lead them to be in that spot. The man took a second to take it all in.

"Your son has the plague? I'm here for the same reason. My daughter had plague-like symptoms. I tried to treat her with some antibiotics I had managed to hide away, but I had no success. The antibiotics had no effect, and I didn't have the lab equipment to figure out why."

"I'm so sorry," Britt said holding back her tears. "How is your daughter doing now?"

"Unfortunately, she passed before I could help her. I guess I should count myself lucky, she went before those doctors could take her away." He looked at Britt. "I'm sorry, I shouldn't have said that."

Adi cut in before Britt could reply.

"So, is that what brought you here? To stop the same thing from happening to other people?"

"In a way," he took off his shoes and socks, and showed his blackening toes. "I'm pretty sure I have it too. I came to see why the antibiotics I had weren't effective and hopefully come up with something that can save me.."

There was an awkward pause, as no one was quite sure what to say when faced with a plague-blackened toe. Then Adi broke the silence. "I've just realized, we've shared all this, but we don't even know your name yet. Hi. I'm Adi, this is Britt," he said as he extended his hand.

"I'm Charles."

"Well Charles, we can't begin to tell you how happy we are to have you here. Let's get to work shall we?"

"Absolutely."

Charles grabbed everything he needed to take a blood sample. He tied off a tourniquet and waited until he saw a pronounced vein to draw from.

"Would you like me to do that?" Britt asked.

"I've taken my own blood countless times for various studies, it's no big deal but thank you." Charles plunged the needle into his vein, used his teeth to untie the rubber tourniquet and watched as his blood filled the vial.

Once the vial was filled, Charles slowly pulled the needle from his arm and extracted the vial from the syringe.

"Well, the easy part's over."

Charles walked over to a microscope. He placed the vial in a stand then walked over to the pile of books Adi had gathered. He picked one up, flipped through the pages and found what he was looking for. A diagram of what the bubonic plague looked like. Placing the book beside the microscope he found a slide and dropped a small drop of his blood on it. Once he was satisfied he had enough of a sample to analyze, he slid it under the lens. He looked through the eyepiece then at the textbook and back into the eyepiece.

"Hmm," was followed closely by "interesting, very interesting."

He picked up the book and rapidly flipped through the pages. He stopped and stared at this page, then back into the eyepiece. He looked at the book again and then flipped back to the original page for the plague.

"Okay, so this is interesting. It appears that I am not infected with the traditional Bubonic Plague, but rather a super plague. Years of treating everything with antibiotics and adding them to our food supply has killed the weakest bacteria, leaving only the strongest to survive and evolve. The plague had to morph to survive."

"Oh, that's what James meant when he said the original recipe just won't work," Britt said to Adi.

"What?" Charles asked.

"We had the last remaining scientists here analyze a sample we brought them, that was the last thing they said on the phone before they disappeared. My guess is they were saying regular antibiotics won't work," Britt clarified.

"I don't know about that, but that is the correct summation of what is happening here. Normal antibiotics won't do it. This is unlike anything I've ever seen. It will take me some time to come up with something." Charles turned to look into the microscope again, then paused. "Say, by the way, if we do come up with something that will work, how do you propose you'll get it to your son?"

"I'm glad you asked," Adi said with an eager tone in his voice. He then went into Britt's plan. It was clear to her that they both thought she was crazy, but neither could find a better alternative solution to the problem. All three were very intelligent, but none of them had much experience dealing with supernatural events. Then Charles asked a question they didn't know was a problem.

"How are you going to get past the guys out front, blocking the entrance?"

"What?" Britt asked. "We just walked right in. How many are out there?"

"It looked like just two. At least it was just the two I ran into, that chased me down the hall."

"We will need some sort of distraction," Adi said. "Maybe if I run and make a lot of noise, they'll chase me."

"No, I'll do it," Charles volunteered.

"If this works, we'll need you here making the vaccinations and cures," Adi said. "It has to be me. Britt needs to go get her son, you need to make the antibiotics."

"We don't need to worry about any of that right now. Once I figure out the process, I'll write it down step by step and you can make some while I'm here. You can do this. Trust me." Charles suggested that Adi and Britton rest while he did his research. He said he would wake them when it came time to start mixing formulas. They wanted to argue with him, but they were both exhausted from the past few days, so they found a quiet corner and tried their best to sleep.

The pair woke to the sound of glass smashing on the floor. They jumped to their feet. Adi, in a haze, mumbled, "What, what's going on?"

Charles laughed, "Sorry to have woken you, I think I am on to something exciting here."

He was surrounded by several open textbooks, pieces of equipment and several bottles of various fluids and other ingredients.

"At home, I was limited with the type and strength of antibiotics I could use to treat Autumn, but I don't have the limitation here. I started off with the standard antibiotics in a much stronger dosage than recommended. They didn't work any better than they did at home. I was starting to get disillusioned, but I remembered a study in the late 2010s before all this went down, they were starting to use a mixture of vaccination with antibiotics to treat urinary tract infections that have become immune to standard antibiotics. That got me to think about plague vaccinations. Although not very popular here in the U.S., even before the ban, they were used in other countries with a higher risk of coming into contact with the plague. I started to play around with the different key components. I started with Y. pestis which are themselves antimicrobics resistant organisms."

"Sure, sure," Adi nodded in agreement, with a facial expression that clearly showed that he did not have a clue what Charles was saying.

Charles continued, "I still have some work to do to fine tune the formula, but so far things look good, have a look."

Charles pushed the microscope towards Adi and Britt. They both saw his infected blood prior to the treatment on the first slide. On the second, the blood after treatment was beginning to look more normal.

"Promising, no?" Charles asked.

"Sure, sure." Adi repeated.

"How long were we asleep for?" Britton asked.

"Not long, I already had a plan, mixing the formula doesn't take a lot of time. Collecting the material was what took the time."

"Great, well, what can we do to help?" Britt asked.

"I have pretty much everything I need now, I just need to fine tune the formula. I suggest you guys work out how you're going to find the plague doctors, and where they'll be when you're ready to try your plan."

"Right," Adi said, with an air of disappointment in his voice. Adi didn't want to sit on the bench, he wanted to be right there with Charles, but he knew Charles was more than capable of finding a solution on his own.

"That's simple," Britton said. "We'll just watch the news and see who reports flowers missing."

"Exactly what I was thinking," Charles agreed.

"Okay, sounds easy enough," Adi said, and they used Charles' phone to look at all the news sites in and around Atlanta.

"I have no idea who these guys are or how this works. I think I should be closer to home before I attempt to make contact, just in case you end up in different locations when you go through the fog." Britton said. They both reluctantly agreed.

"Should one of us go with you?" Adi asked.

"No, you two work here, I'll get back home okay. You just get enough together so that if I make it there and back, we have enough for everyone. Or at least as many as possible."

Charles worked as Adi watched over his shoulder, trying to learn as much as he could. Britt scoured the internet looking for stories of destroyed flower beds close to her house. Several hours passed and they were all showing signs of fatigue when Charles leaned back from the microscope, proclaiming, "I think I have it!"

"What? Really?" Britt asked excitedly.

"I think so, what do you think?" Charles moved out of the way so Adi could look through the eyepiece.

"By George, I think that's it."

Britt ran over and took a look. "It looks almost normal."

"The contents of the vaccination will alter the blood cells slightly, but that's to be expected. I think all we need to do now is to actually try it."

"Are you sure you're ready?" Britt asked.

"Well, we are running out of time, and I think, given the resources and time constraints, it's our only option."

"If you're sure."

"I am." Charles confirmed. He transposed his notes to something more legible. He showed them to Adi. "Can you read this?"

"I can."

"Okay, I'm going to make a batch big enough for a sample, watch very closely." Charles proceeded to mix the formula together while Adi watched and made his own notes. Finally, there was enough in a syringe for Charles to inject himself.

"Well, here goes nothing," he said with a smile as he sunk the needle into his upper arm and depressed the plunger. "Okay so far so good. Now we wait."

"How long until you'll know if it worked or not?" Adi asked.

"It could take up to 12 hours to make a visible difference in my blood, and 24 hours or more to start making a physical difference."

They decided they would wait 24 hours to make sure there were no immediate side effects of the new vaccination. They were hoping that if any serious complications showed up after 24 hours, Britt and Hunter would be home and they could treat it then.

Charles talked more about his family, mentioning that his wife had passed away during childbirth, so he had raised Autumn alone. Although he eluded to volunteering to be the distraction because he didn't care if he came back or not, he never fully said it out loud. Adi and Britt continued to talk like Charles would get back unscathed after running his distraction.

At the end of the 24 hours, Charles did a full check-up to examine how well the vaccination had worked. He said he was feeling better with more energy. He took his temperature, monitored his heart rate, and drew another blood sample. He looked under the microscope. "Looks good. I think we have it, or at least something that will make him strong enough to get home.

"Okay, we'll go tonight, when the guards will be tired and not expecting anyone coming from the building," Britt said.

It was one a.m. when they decided to make their move. First, Britt crawled through the door, as quietly as possible. She opened the door to the hallway ever so gingerly, and looked. Confident they were alone, at least in that part of the building, Charles followed her out. The pair stayed together as they navigated their way in the dark to the main entrance.

"Okay, game time," Charles said.

Britt got the impression that he was loving this excitement. She hid as Charles opened the outside door and quietly walked along the edge of the building, using bushes for cover. He got as far away from the front door as he could go, but still be seen by the guards. He threw a rock in their direction, but it didn't come close enough for them to notice. He yelled, and once they looked in his direction, he bolted. They ran after him. So far the plan was working.

Britt walked along the outside of the building in the opposite direction, and once she was out of the light of the main entrance, she ran towards the road. There she started to walk casually, like she was just some other person on her way to who knows where. She knew she wasn't in the clear, but she tried to look as relaxed as possible. That was, until she heard the automatic gunfire. She stepped up her pace a bit and prayed the shots were just a warning.

Several minutes later, she got to the garage and found the hearse. She was happy it was still there and it didn't look like it had been tampered with. She had no reason to think the car was being watched. She jumped in, turned the key and the car once again came to life. The hole in the muffler made the car louder than she wanted, but she figured she was far enough away that the loud noise wouldn't sound any alarms. After all, cars were still legal.

After the 11 hour drive home from the CDC she decided not to drive past her house. She thought it would definitely be under surveillance, so she stopped at a neighbouring town, paid cash for a motel that didn't look like it would be too suspicious of a single woman checking in by herself and took the opportunity to catch up on some sleep.

Her sleep wasn't a long one, or an overly refreshing one, because no matter how hard she tried, she couldn't take her mind off the task at hand, or stop herself from imagining the horrors Hunter was going through, if he was still alive.

When she woke up, she started looking all over the news. She was reluctant to post a question, in case her name was flagged. She was just hoping missing flowers were still newsworthy.

It wasn't long before she found what she was looking for. A group of elderly women were complaining about the lack of respect of today's youth, destroying a community flower garden. The town they were describing wasn't far from where she was. The plague doctors typically appeared in the darkness of the night so she paced around her room until it was late enough that she could get ready without drawing a lot of attention. She gathered her things and drove over.

She got there at dusk. She had time to figure out the most likely place the "doctors" would show up. She stopped to get gas, and asked if there was a hospital or health clinic around. The attendant said there were no hospitals, but a local gym was being used as a makeshift clinic where many of the town's sick were being cared for. She thought that was her best option.

She went to the gym and parked. She didn't get many dirty looks for sitting in a hearse. Because the rampant diseases led to many deaths, hearse sightings weren't as rare as they used to be.

Britt gathered the gear she 'borrowed' from the museum and put on most of it. She didn't want to get any more attention than she already had, and if anyone saw her dressed as a plague doctor, she would likely be accused of being with the group that was dragging people away.

It was now a waiting game.

Britt sat upright. The clock on the dash read 1:49 a.m. The temperature had dropped considerably and a fog rolled in. The fog was thick and reduced visibility to zero. She heard footsteps walking right next to her car. She finished getting dressed in her uniform, putting the mask on last. The smell of the old leather almost made her gag, but she kept going. She stepped out of the car just as the fog lifted and she saw the last couple of doctors enter the gym. Like the other times, there was screaming and people tried to stop them, but they just walked right past them. She had no idea how many doctors entered the room but her plan was to hide in front of the car and hopefully follow the last one back into the fog.

She didn't have to wait long, the doctors began to re-emerge out of the gym just as the fog returned. Britt took a deep breath and despite losing visibility, did her best to gauge when she needed to join them. She stood up, walked up behind the last leather coat she saw and got as close as she could. They kept walking. This time when the fog lifted, the doctors and the sick were still visible. She wasn't sure if she had been successful or not, until she turned around to look at the gym. It was gone. The last of the fog disappeared and as Britt was trying to get her bearings, a horrific smell made her ill. It smelt like feces and rotting flesh. Being an undertaker, she was well aware of what a rotting corpse smelt like but in all her experience, the smell had never been as extreme as this.

She pulled up her mask and began vomiting. When she stopped, she noticed a small group of doctors looking at her. It was attention she didn't want. One of them walked up to her, grabbed the beak of her mask and pulled it down saying, "Miasma." She kept her eyes down to avoid looking at the man, in case he realized she wasn't one of them.

It was then she actually looked around and registered where she was. It looked like the illustrations in her textbooks. There were 14th-century tents scattered all over the land, body parts stacked up in piles according to limb, and there was a large fire with several doctors throwing bodies and body parts in. It was at this point she heard the screams.

There were loud shrills of people being tortured. She walked around the encampment without being noticed. She was just one of over a hundred plague doctors all walking around taking care of their business. She looked behind the flaps of the tents, each one had about a dozen patients, all with doctors performing surgeries. The tents were leather, the medical equipment they were using were all hand tools, and barbaric by modern standards. She looked in one tent that had the loudest screams emitting from it. She made eye contact with a person on the table, he was screaming as the doctors used a handsaw to remove his polyp covered arm.

Britt was still trying to make sense of what she was seeing as the urgency to find her son grew. She couldn't let the thought even cross her mind that her son could be one of the bodies in a pile, or the bones amongst the ashes.

The more panicked she got, the clumsier she got, which in turn drew her more attention. A few doctors were looking at her, a couple started walking in her direction. She turned and ran. There was no end in sight. The bodies, the tents, the smell, they went on for miles. She was once again beginning to think it was going to be useless.

She turned a corner and saw a few tents in a more secluded area. The sounds and smells lessened. She saw something she wasn't prepared to see. It was a pile of clothes that belonged to kids. She knew she was close, and that he was still alive. She felt it to her core. She opened a few tent flaps. The doctors took a quick glance at her, but then went back to caring for the children. They weren't doing amputations or any other medical treatments on them. She wasn't sure why. Maybe it was because they felt kids couldn't tolerate the treatment, so they just kept them comfortable while they got sicker and sicker. Some of the kids that that were in the final stages of the plague were crying and tossing on the straw-filled mats they were given. Some kids were dressed in modern clothes, others were dressed in clothes more suited for the fourteenth century. She thought it was odd that the old clothes were in great condition, like the tents, the equipment and the doctors themselves, it was like she was actually in the 1300s, but she couldn't stop to think about it, she had to find Hunter.

As dawn approached, she was worried they would either disappear in the sunlight or they would notice she wasn't like the rest of them. After all, her uniform looked 700 years old, while theirs looked fresh out of the box. It was then, as the sun started to rise, she opened a tent and saw Hunter lying on a straw-filled mat, in obvious pain but alone, with no doctors around him. She walked over to him. He looked up and screamed, "MOM!"

The doctors that were in the tent attending to other kids looked at her. She didn't care, she pulled off her mask and gave her son a hug. The doctors all started walking towards her and an alarm was raised. She knew she had only seconds. She pulled out the syringe, shoved it in Hunter's arm and pressed the plunger.

The doctors grabbed her and started saying "miasma" over and over again. One picked up her mask off the floor and before putting it back on her, he inspected it, obviously confused as to why it was aged like it was. The other doctors noticed she was a woman. They stepped back, looked at each other and then reached for her. She tried to fight them off, but they were used to dealing with uncooperative patients. They put the mask over her head, tore away her bag containing the other syringes and the Anglo-Saxon dictionary she brought with her, and dragged out, her kicking and screaming. She reached out for Hunter, and he reached for her to no avail. She could hear him screaming for her. She didn't know where they were taking her or what they were going to do to her, and she didn't care. She was only worried about Hunter.

They dragged her for what felt like an eternity. Eventually they reached the flaps of a tent on the outer edge of their makeshift village. One of the doctors went into the tent, while the other stayed with Britt. Britt could hear something going on in the tent, but she couldn't make it out. Their words sounded distorted as they spoke through the masks they were wearing. She could hear the odd word clearly but it didn't sound like English. The short video she watched with Ray, the paranormal-store owner, wasn't nearly enough to make her an authority on the Anglo-Saxon language she hoped they were speaking.

Before long, the flap opened. The doctor said something and Britt's escort pushed her into the tent. The tent looked like a command post of sorts, where the top doctors were discussing how to treat the ill. At the front of the tent was a doctor in a grey plague suit. Britt's escort pushed her into a chair while the others tried to ask her questions. She couldn't understand what they were saying, nor could they understand her. They all thought she was talking nonsense and treated it like a symptom. Britt tried her best to point to her bag so she could get her book or at least to show them the needles, to explain who she was and what she was doing there, but nothing worked.

She tried to tell them that the plague wasn't airborne, she was channeling her inner charades champion, but even with her diagrams and acting skills, nothing was getting through to them. The harder she tried, the more frantic she looked. Eventually, four more doctors walked in, and when she turned to look at the new arrivals, she was grabbed from behind. They extended her arms and slid a straitjacket over her head. She continued to struggle and plead her case as they dragged her away. They dragged her to another tent across the compound. They opened the flap and tossed her in. Inside were other patients that the doctors had diagnosed as insane.

Her tent mates screamed and cried all throughout the day and night, which barely masked the sounds of the other screams echoing across the air. After she was placed in the tent she was fed a small amount of some porridge-type food. They shoved it in her face and she had to fight to get even a little bit in her mouth. They went around to all the patients feeding them in that fashion. She wasn't given a mat, so she was just expected to sleep on the ground they were sitting on. They also didn't get any bathroom breaks. The other patients were covered in their own waste, which attracted flies and rodents. All she could do was cry as she tried to figure out her next move.

While the others were sleeping, she struggled to get loose of her jacket, but she couldn't. She began to wish she had watched more magicians while she could. Her tent mates were just as distorted as the others when they talked, all but one that was. She sat quietly in a corner. Britt noticed her early on and assumed she was catatonic. All day she just sat perfectly still, staring at the tent flap. She didn't move when doctors came and went, she didn't move when they were trying to feed her. She barely blinked.

Britt was trying to keep her emotions in check so she could think and plan. She also hoped they would see that she wasn't crazy. At the end of the day, they came in and dimmed the lanterns. Britt struggled to get comfortable on the ground and let out a couple curse words while she did. It was then the woman in the corner said something perfectly intelligible. "The best way is to lie on your back."

Britt struggled to sit up. She looked at the woman. Britt wasn't sure if she had actually heard the woman speak, or if she was truly going crazy.

The woman looked back at her. "Nothing really works, the back is the best if you can."

"Can you understand me?" Britt asked, puzzled.

"Yes, I'm one of you. From your time."

"From my time? Where are we, what is this place?"

Britt was 98% sure she knew she was in the 1300s, but she wanted to hear someone else say it first.

"You haven't figured it out yet? We went back in time. That fog, it brought us here."

"I mean, ya, I thought that's what happened, but then I thought maybe I really was crazy. How is this even possible?"

"I don't know. I was working at a hospital and these guys came in one night and started to drag off one of my patients. I chased after them, into that fog and when it disappeared, I was here. I assume they hear us like we hear them, distorted and weird. I guess they think we're speaking in gibberish. How did you get here?"

"They took my son…"

"Oh. Did you find him or is he…gone?"

"No, he's here, I found him and gave him a shot before they dragged me here. How do we get home?" Britt asked.

"Home. Ha. This is home now, unless you can master time travel."

"I managed to get here, I can get us home." Britt said, confidently.

"You came here…on purpose?"

"I told you, they have my son. I wasn't going to just let him go."

Britt explained her plan of how she got there. She told the nurse about Adi and Charles, and their vaccinations. While they were talking, they shuffled closer together, and leaned up against each other, using each other as support as they tried to sleep.

Britt fell to the ground as her new friend was dragged off. Britt tried to ask where they were taking her. The doctors ignored her and her friend was just screaming for help. Britt had no idea how long she was gone for, but the sun was setting by the time they brought her back. When they did, she had blood dripping from her eyes and drool dangling from her lips. Britton tried talking to her but it was useless. The lobotomy was too effective. Britton noticed the doctors talking and looking at Britt. She began to panic, thinking she was the next up for a lobotomy. The doctors looked out at the setting sun and left the tent. Britt assumed she had until morning to figure out how to get free, find Hunter again and get back to her own time.

Her efforts throughout the night were fruitless. The dawn brought the doctors into the tent. Despite her efforts, they carried her away with ease. They took her to another tent that contained a wooden table with grooves around the edge. She knew exactly what it was and she was now in full panic. With her arms entangled in her straitjacket, the doctors easily held her down to the table. Her head was kept in place by a thick leather strap. A doctor approached her with two long metal prongs, another doctor pried her eyelids open. Britt felt the cold, unsterilized steel touch her eyeball just as another doctor came rushing into the tent.

The doctors talked for a bit, then in a huff, the doctor about to treat her tossed his instruments on the table and hoisted her up to a sitting position. They dragged Britt across the compound. The morning sun illuminated the massive treatment area. There were tents and people as far as she could see in any direction. The site was even worse in the daylight. There was blood and human waste everywhere. The piles of bodies, body parts and the ash of what used to be human was in a much larger scale than she first imagined. She didn't even want to hazard a guess as to how many bodies had died in that area alone.

Britt kept strong. She wanted to be strong for Hunter, but she also wanted to be as composed as possible in case they were re-evaluating her mental state. She got nervous as she rounded a corner to an area she was familiar with. It was the area with all the children, including her son. Her legs began to get weak, her mind was racing a mile a minute. She was excited at the prospect of seeing her son, but afraid of what the reunion could mean for both of them.

Britton and her escorts reached the tent she thought Hunter was in. When they opened the flap, she saw the same doctor in the white suit that had sentenced her to her lobotomy. Hunter was nowhere to be seen. Britt looked around frantically, then the doctor looked at her and began to speak. Britt couldn't understand him, until he stepped aside and saw Hunter sitting in a chair. He looked tired and still a bit weak, but he looked much better than he had the night he was taken from her. Hunter saw his mom and ran over to her. He wrapped his arms around her. She wished she could do the same, but she was still in the straitjacket. The doctor in white said something else to one of her escorts, and he began to undo her jacket. As soon as the jacket fell to the ground, Britt stretched then gave her son a huge hug. She asked Hunter if he was okay, if they did anything to him. He said he was scared and hungry.

The doctor began to speak again. Britt understood he was asking her a question. She made the assumption it was how she made Hunter get better. She spoke as slowly and clearly as possible, using charades and diagrams to convey her message. She tried to explain to him about the needles, the vaccination, and about her being a time traveller. She had no idea how she'd get that last point across so she just focused on the medication. All the doctors wore a medical kit around their chest. She pointed to it, then to herself. The doctor nodded and gave a command to another doctor. After a few minutes, he returned with her bag. She was relieved that they were slowly starting to communicate.

Britt reached into her bag and pulled out another syringe full of the cure and the dictionary Ray had so graciously loaned to her. She showed the needle to the doctors, then demonstrated how it worked on another child from her own time period, then the head doctor injected one of the children. She remembered Adi's words telling her not to influence the past to change the future. Since she was working on the assumption the doctors were restless souls, she made the natural leap the other patients from their time were also dead, so she wasn't worried about altering the past and she hoped that as the dead got better, they may all be able to finally rest in peace. She also hoped that as they gave the shots to those from her time, they would be returned to where they were taken from. All this was speculation but speculation was all she had. It's not like they have literature on how to deal with ghost doctors.

As she rummaged through her bag, she realized there was one syringe missing. She knew she had had five on her when she left Atlanta, but now she could only find four. After Hunter, her demonstration on a patient and the doctor's trial, they only had one left. The doctor in white gave the last syringe to another doctor. He injected another child and they were out.

The doctor in white started asking Britt a question. She understood just enough to know he was asking if she had more. Britton began flipping through her book, but because it was a dictionary of Anglo-Saxon words, she needed to know the word before she could find the definition. Reverse engineering it to find the word by using the definition was proving to be too difficult. She tossed the book on a table and used diagrams and exaggerated gestures to tell him who she was, where they were from and her idea to get them home. The explanation took a very long time and she was certain the doctor didn't understand most of it, especially when he nodded to one of the other doctors, who picked up the jacket again. Hunter jumped in front of his mother to protect her. The doctor holding the jacket paused, the doctor in white said something, and the other doctor walked out of the tent, with the jacket.

Another doctor picked up the book and began flipping through the pages. He then said something to the head doctor and showed him the book. The doctor in white looked over some pages then up at Britt. The two doctors talked for a bit before pointing at word in the book, then to his mask. Britt looked at the book and of course the word they had pointed out was the only one she understood. "Miasma."

Britt read the word aloud then shook her head no. She then tried to act like a rat, the doctor nodded and flipped through the dictionary to the Anglo-Saxon word for rat. Britt smiled and nodded then mimicked a flea and the doctor found the correct word. She then tried to tell them the plague came from the fleas. She wasn't sure if the message was getting through, especially when the doctor cut her off.

He began to draw a map on the ground, Britt recognized it as a map to where she first arrived. He then handed Britt a candle with a mark on it. The doctor pointed at the notch in the candle then down at the ground. He then put the candle in a lantern and lit it. The doctor flipped through the book and pointed to the word dægmæl which meant "clock." Britt understood it to mean that she and Hunter needed to be at that place when the candle burnt down to the notch. Finally, he handed Britt and Hunter masks, and although she knew the plague wasn't airborne, they still filled their masks up with flowers just to kill the horrific smell. She then blindfolded Hunter so he wouldn't see the death that was surrounding them.

They had plenty of time before they had to go to the meeting spot so Britt went to rescue her friend. She knew that even after the lobotomy, she would be better off in her own time with modern medicine than she would being stuck in the 1300s forever.

Just as Britt made it to the tent, she saw two Plague Doctors dragging a body out towards the fire. Britt ran up to them. She looked at the body and it was her new friend. Britt wanted to cry but she stayed strong. Before she let them throw her on the fire, she ripped her necklace off. She hoped that someone back in her time would recognize it and get some closure.

When the candle was nearing the notch, the white doctor showed up with some other doctors. He tried to speak to Britton. Through rudimentary drawings on the ground, she hoped the doctor understood that she would be back in a week with more supplies to help their sick. The doctor nodded and the sky turned black, the fogged rolled in, surrounding Britt and her son. When the fog lifted, they were back at the gym she had left from.

Ignoring all the people gathered around, and the police approaching her, she and Hunter jumped in the hearse and started to head back to Atlanta. She was relieved Hunter was home, and appeared to be on the mend. Now they needed to get back to Adi and Charles. She turned on the radio to ease the combined tension and boredom of the long trip.

A news bulletin came on, announcing that the President was sick. He was getting polyps and a fever. The announcer gave out a number asking anyone who could help to call. She knew it was the plague, and for a second was happy that karma was catching up with him. Then, out came the compassionate person she really was. She decided she'd just swing by the CDC to make sure Adi and Charles were still safe. If she could make it past the guards to get more of the vaccine, she would then go and save the president. She had no idea how she would do all of this.

As she slowed the car to stop at a red light, a syringe rolled out from under the seat of the car. She had apparently dropped it in her haste. She looked at it briefly, and decided she would go to Washington first, since it was on her way.

When they got to Washington, Britt found a convenience store roughly two miles from the White House. She went inside and bought a pay-as-you-go phone. Once she was back in the car, Hunter handed her the piece of paper, where he had written the number from the radio. Britt called and she was surprised when a voice answered, "Hello, White House."

Britt was so amazed she had reached a real person, she almost gave her name. Catching herself, she skipped over the pleasantries and went right into it.

"Can you get me in touch with the people caring for the president? I know what he has and I have a cure."

The operator started to tell her to come to the White House when Britt cut her off.

"There is no way I'm going there. I've seen what your people do to people like me. It's a crime to have what I have. I'm not going to let you kill me just to save that asshole. I need assurances."

"Of course ma'am. What kind of assurances would you need?"

"The kind I'm sure you're not authorized to make. Can you transfer me to someone closer to the president?" Britt demanded.

"Ma'am, we're getting hundreds of calls a day, including death threats, how do we know..."

Britt cut her off. "He has the plague. I'm the woman that came back through the fog with my son."

She was sure she had made the news, or at least had the President's spies report to him about her.

"Hold on a moment please."

"Hello, this is the President's personal physician, I hear you may have a cure for us?" a new voice asked sternly.

"Not so fast. How do I know I'll be safe? That my son and I will make it out of there alive?" she asked.

"You have our word."

Britt laughed, "And that's worth so much."

"The President is dying ma'am. He won't last much longer. He needs you."

"That is hardly a promise. After I give him the shot, he'll bounce back and I'll be trapped."

The doctor asked, "Before we agree to anything, where did you get this magic cure?"

"I'm not saying another word. You know who I am. You know I'm for real. If he wants my help, he will have to meet my demands or you will never hear from me again," Britt said, matter of factly.

"Hold on a moment please."

As Britt was on hold, she began to get nervous. She was watching plain black SUVs drive by, and anyone walking by that happened to look in her direction had her on edge. She was just about to drive away to save herself and her son when the doctor came back onto the line.

"Okay, the President will hear you out. Can you come to the White House?"

"It may take me some time to get there. Before I agree to anything, I want to be met at the front gate with a news van who will be broadcasting live. When we meet with the President he must support vaccinations, rescind 2028-45, as well as his plenary powers, and step down as President. Live, on TV. He must sign a contract and the reporter that comes with me gets a copy."

The doctor paused for a few minutes before responding, "Okay, hold please."

Very little time passed before the line opened again.

"The president agrees to your terms. We will have everything ready for you when you get here."

"Like I said, it may take me a bit to get there, I'm..."

This time the doctor cut her off.

"It shouldn't take you too long to drive two miles in an old hearse, Ms. Gravel."

Britton panicked. She tossed the phone out the window and sped off. She was close to hyperventilating.

"What's wrong, Mom?" Hunter asked.

"Nothing honey, I just had a bit of a scare. Now hold on, I need to think."

She began to have a back and forth with herself. "He knows who I am. Where I am. If he wanted me dead, he could just come take the cure along with Hunter and me. Maybe he's telling the truth? What do I have to lose now? Just my life and Hunters. What about Adi? What happens to him if I disappear? How do I know he's still alive? Fuck. Okay, I can change the world or I can be the biggest sucker on the planet. Can I make it to Atlanta to leave Hunter with Adi? No, that's stupid, that's just as dangerous if not more so. I don't even know if Adi is still alive. Okay, we'll go. They won't kill us on live TV would they? Maybe as a warning. They've done it before. But why wait until now? Why pretend the president is sick just to get me? They already know where I am. Okay, we'll go."

"What are you saying, Mom?" Hunter asked, not being able to make out a word she had said.

"We're going to the White House to meet the president…I hope."

A few minutes later, Britton pulled up to the gates of the White House and stopped. She instantly regretted her decision to meet with the President, as a group of security personnel surrounded her car. Without speaking to her, a guard with a dog walked around her car, while another used a mirror to inspect the undercarriage. Without warning, a young agent opened the door and sat in the passenger seat of her hearse, nudging Hunter to the middle of the bench seat.

"Ms. Gravel I assume?"

"Yes. Can you please tell me what's going on?" Britton asked.

"Just some precautions. Okay, now we're going to drive up the lane to a garage behind the building for further security checks," the agent said with a serious tone.

"Ya, right. This isn't what I agreed to. Look, I want to talk to the Dr…"

"The doctor is in the garage waiting for you. Once we get there, you and your son will be checked, the vial will be checked and if you clear, you will go see the President."

"No, I'm not moving until the press is here," Britton told the Agent.

"I've been told they're on their way. DRIVE MA'AM," the agent said sternly.

"I'm sure they are," Britton's words to the agent were dripping with sarcasm. "Hold on Hunter, you'll be okay."

Britt put the old car into gear and pressed the accelerator. Up ahead, she could see more agents in suits and a man in a white lab coat. When Britt stopped the car, agents opened the doors and pulled her and Hunter out. One agent patted her down as the doctor approached.

"Hello, I'm Dr. …"

"Ya, I know who you are. You're the one I talked to on the phone."

"Yes, that is correct Ms. Gravel. I am the one you spoke to on the phone."

"Well Doctor. This isn't what we agreed to."

"I am aware, I'm terribly sorry. The Secret Service rarely takes a doctors opinion when it comes to the safety of the President."

"I'm out of here. Let me go," Britton demanded.

"Relax. Everything else is on schedule. The President's lawyer is drafting up his resignation papers and a new executive order rescinding 2028-45, just as you asked. And look," the doctor nodded in the direction of the main gate. "The media is here. You have nothing to worry about. The press secretary will brief the rest of the media while this team escorts you to visit the President. The President asks just one thing."

"Of course," she said, sarcastically. "What is it?"

"The President would like this to sound like his idea. That he secretly put you and a team of scientists together to work on a cure, and he got himself sick to be the guinea pig. He will step down, he just wants to step down as a hero."

"Whatever. As long as his reign of terror is over. Do you think anyone will buy it?" she asked, nodding in the direction of the camera crew setting up.

"Honestly, probably not, but it doesn't matter if they do. It's the only way he'll agree to step down."

The doctor escorted Britton and Hunter into the White House, with the camera crew and Secret Service agents behind them. They walked through a garage area to an elevator. They couldn't all squeeze into one car, so the doctor told an agent to stay with the camera crew and wait for the second car. Britt was now separated from her live camera safety net. She became unsettled as they rode up to see the President, but it all happened so fast, she didn't have the opportunity to exit the elevator or voice her objections.

The Secret Service agents escorted them through the corridors to the President's room where two more agents were waiting for them. One of the agents opened the door. The doctor, Britton and Hunter entered. The Vice President was standing beside the President.

An agent made the introductions. "President McBride, Vice President Bowman, may I introduce Ms. Britton Gravel?"

"Thank you for coming Ms. Gravel. May I have the antidote please?" the President asked from his bed.

"It's not an antidote. You weren't poisoned, you have the plague. I have a cure here in my bag."

"Look, I don't care what you call it, give it to me."

"Not until the media gets here. We made a deal."

"I'm sorry Ms. Gravel, I've been told there is a problem with the elevator. The media won't be here for a bit. They're working on it."

"Of course," Britt said with her heart sinking. She knew she had made a huge mistake.

"Now, may I please have your cure?"

"No, not until the media gets her," Britt said, trying to stay strong for Hunter.

"Gentlemen," President McBride said, nodding to the Secret Service agents. Two men stepped towards Britton. They grabbed her and one ripped her bag from her grip. He rummaged through her bag. He found the syringe and handed it to the President's doctor. The doctor handed it off to another agent who took it and ran out of the room. Britton assumed they were going to make sure it wasn't poison.

"Thank you Ms. Gravel, you're dismissed."

The President nodded to the agent holding her. He began to pull her and Hunter towards the door.

The Vice President stepped up.

"Enough George, it's over. Let her go."

The President shifted in his bed to make eye contact with Bowman.

"You insolent ass. Who do you think you are? You don't think you can be replaced?"

The President gestured to the agent that took the bag. "You can take the Vice President with Ms. Gravel and her son."

As the agent approached the Vice president, the agents protecting Bowman stepped in front of him. The President's men drew their weapons and stared hard at the other agents, who also drew their weapons. Britt put her hand on Hunter's chest and they both stepped back out of the line of fire, as she struggled to understand what was going on.

"George, ENOUGH. It's over. The media will be through that door in about 10 seconds. How do you want this handled? Do you want them to see us like this, or do you want to go out with your original plan where you try to come off like a hero?"

"What is going on here? You want my job, is that it?" McBride asked, defiantly.

"Listen you idiot. I took this job to minimize the damage your narcissistic ass is causing. For the last year, I've been working with the secret service agents I trust the most. We've been taking the scientists and whoever else you arrested under 2028-45, and we've had them working in a lab in an old nuclear fallout shelter. It was only a matter of time before we had enough power to overthrow you. Your illness and Ms. Gravel's arrival was perfect timing for us. We are taking this country back. We can shoot it out or you can give up. Which is it? The media is right outside."

The agents defending the president looked at each other, and then to the agents standing with the Vice President. They holstered their weapons. Bowman's security detail followed suit. The President knew he didn't have an ally in the room.

There was a knock on the door.

"They're here," said Bowman. "What will it be, Mr. President?"

With a deep sigh, President McBride gave up.

"Ok, you win Dan. I'll honour my original deal with Ms. Gravel."

Vice President Bowman nodded to the agent closest to the door. The agent stepped towards the door and opened it. The media came in with the lab worker, who handed the doctor the vial.

"Sir, we analyzed it and it doesn't contain anything lethal, but that was a very quick analysis, it will take some time to do a complete breakdown."

Britt impatiently interrupted.

"For fucks sake, if I wanted him to die, I would have let nature take its course. What would I have to gain by killing a dying man? Inject some into me if you want," she said, as she extended her arm.

President McBride, looking into the camera.

"No, that's okay. How can I not trust Ms. Gravel? After all, we've been working together for some time to get this medicine ready for mass production."

Britt tried to hold back making gagging sounds as he spoke.

The President continued speaking to the camera.

"I've asked Ms. Gravel to join me today to make a very special announcement. As many of you may or may not know, I have recently come down with an illness. That illness is the Black Plague. As many Americans were coming down with the same illness and being taken away into the fog, I employed a very small group of people to work around the clock to identify the illness and make a cure. Right now, that cure is in a very small trial basis, and to prove my commitment to the American People, I have volunteered to be the first to take this new medicine."

The doctor looked at Britt. She nodded at him, and he injected the needle into the president's arm. The President winced, and then coughed a couple of times.

"See America. There is nothing to fear from modern medicine. In fact, we need to rely on it for the survival of our great nation. Over the last few years, we've had some serious setbacks. Through my leadership, we were able to work past them to where we are today. Over the coming weeks and months, we will see a resurgence in medicine. Which leads me to my next point."

The president grabbed a binder from the table beside him.

"This is executive order 2045-10. This order rescinds 2028-45 and removes all of its powers and rescinds my pelinary power. Our faith is now restored in our medical professionals, and in their vaccinations and cures. I am living proof of their successes. Because I feel the national emergency is officially over, I will be stepping down as President of these United States of America. We will begin talks to determine the soonest opportunity to hold an election, but for now, I will be transferring all of my power over Vice President Bowman. Thank you, America."

The camera kept recording as the President signed several documents, removing himself as President and putting an end to many of his Presidential decrees. The President then turned to Britton.

"Thank you Ms. Gravel. If it wasn't for you, I know I would be a goner. I know you took a great risk coming here to help me. If there is anything I can do for you, please let me know."

"Well Mr. McBride, thank you for keeping your word. Nothing you can say or do will reverse the damage you've caused over the last 20 years, but this is a good first step towards a better future. As for a favour, I do have one thing I need help with."

"Yes, of course, what is it?" the former President asked.

"If I had friends helping me, would they have immunity?"

"Yes, absolutely! Ah, but that's not my call any more," the President said, looking at the Vice President.

The Vice President replied, "Of course, I will get them working with my team to get everyone on the same page."

"Well, they're currently at the CDC working on making a much bigger batch."

"Impossible. We have security around the building and in it. We would know if someone was working in there," Bowman said.

"Unless you killed them, they're there. Trust me."

"Well, let's go get him, shall we?" President Bowman said as he pointed to the door.

Leaving the former President behind to recuperate, the group walked to the backyard of the White House, where the Marine One helicopter was spooling up. They jumped in and buckled up as the helicopter lifted off. The Camera Operator and Reporter were left on the lawn of the White House.

The agents at the front door of the CDC were surprised to see the helicopter come out of the sky and land beside them. A secret service agent on the helicopter ran over to the two guarding the building. Britton could see them speaking, but the noise of the helicopter made it impossible to hear what they were saying. One of the agents pointed to the building, the two posted out front looked at the building, then shook their heads back and forth.

The agent from the helicopter pointed at them and signalled for them to join him. Britt helped Hunter get out of the helicopter. The new President and two more secret service agents joined them, and they entered the building.

"Lead the way," President Bowman gestured to Britt.

Britt was a bit lost at first, but eventually got them to the door she knew Adi was behind. She opened it up and revealed the cleaner's closet.

"See Sir, just as we said. There is no one here. She is pulling something."

Britt gave the agent a stern look as she walked into the closet, and pushed the walls down. They made a loud crashing sound which startled a very surprised Adi.

"See, I told you he was here. Mr. President, may I introduce Aditya Aggarwal."

"Ya, how about that. Right under your noses," Bowman said to the two secret service agents that had been assigned to the CDC. They looked at each other awkwardly.

"Ummm. Hello Britt. What's happening?" Adi asked with a concerned tone.

Hunter yelled, "ADI" and ran up to give him a hug.

"Hi Buddy," Adi said, hugging Hunter tightly. "Britt?"

"Ya, long story short. I saved Hunter, I had to stop off and save the President. He stepped down, 2028-45 is dead and we have a lot of work to do. Wait, where is Charles?"

"I'm sorry, Britt. He never came back that night. I heard gunfire. I'm not sure if they got him or if he just got spooked and kept running."

"The shift before us reported a shooting, sir. The agents weren't on our side. Unfortunately it happened before we got here, so we couldn't get him to safety. I'm sorry sir," one of the agents said.

"You bastards, he was just trying to help where you guys wouldn't," Adi yelled with frustration.

"We're sorry. We wish we could have stopped them, gotten him to safety, we really do."

"It wasn't these guys, Adi. I'll explain everything. But these guys are on our side," Britt said, putting her arm around Adi's shoulders.

"He was a good man," Adi said, visibly angry and upset.

The new President spoke up to try to break the tension.

"We're sorry. We truly are. Ms. Gravel told us all about his integral role in developing the cure. But we have to put his death behind us. We have a lot of work to do. First, we need to get this place back on its feet."

The group left the building. They were amazed at how fast reporters had scrambled to the CDC. The new President addressed the media.

"Ladies and gentlemen, thank you for coming. I'm sure you're all curious for more information about the former president, his health and his status. We will get to that in time. For now, I have an important announcement to make. As Former President McBride said, Ms. Gravel here was vital in diagnosing the plague and coming up with a cure. Over the next few weeks we will need vaccinations and cures for many illnesses. We would like to officially thank Ms.

Britton Gravel, Mr. Aditya Aggarwal and Mr. Charles… (leans over to Adi, in a whisper) what is his last name?"

Adi was embarrassed that he didn't know. "I'm sorry, I don't know. But his daughter's name was Autumn."

"That's okay son. We would like to thank Charles. In honour of his dedication to finding a cure, though he was too late to save his only daughter, we would like to officially name the law repealing 2028-45 'Autumn's Law'."

President Bowman stepped away from the microphones to a round of applause from the media and went to speak to Britton and Adi.

"I know you guys aren't scientists, but you both have a job here at the CDC or in my administration as we pick up the pieces of the last 20 years."

"I appreciate the offer," Britt said. "I really do, but I can't. I have to go back home. I have a funeral home to run, and a son to raise. But I think you should stay Adi, you are wasting your talents in my basement."

"You're going back there?" Adi was shocked. "They hate you, they treat you so badly. Screw them."

"Someone wise once taught me that people act out when they're scared and have no one to turn too." She rustled Hunter's hair. "Now, you have less than a week to make a huge batch of formula so I can get it to the plague doctors and get our people back. Also, the nation needs some too. Good luck, Adi."

"But who will take care of you back in Aurora? I know you can't survive without me." Adi said, with a jerk in his voice.

"I'll manage somehow. Besides, you're always welcome to visit and we don't have to worry about our phones being tapped anymore. You need bigger and better. You'll do amazing things here."

Adi simply replied, "Bollocks."

One week after Britt returned from the 1300's, she was back at the gym. A group of people helped to unload several huge crates of Charles' cure in the field in which Britt had last seen the Plague Doctors. The group waited from nightfall. By 4 a.m. nothing had happened.

"Damn, I guess they didn't understand," Britt said to herself.

She barely got the words out of her mouth, when the temperature began to drop and an eerie fog rolled in and disappeared just as quickly. There was a lone Doctor in the field next to the crates. Britt had known what to expect, but his rather sudden appearance freaked out the other spectators. The Doctor looked up, it felt like he was making direct eye contact with Britton. He nodded. Britt smiled and nodded back. As she did, the fog rolled in and when it disappeared, so had the doctor and all the supplies.

Over the following days, the sick began returning to their own time with little sign of the plague. They were immediately treated at the hospital for their physical and mental health. Britt read the history books and there was no mention of a magical cure for the plague. She assumed her theory that all the doctors and patients from that era were souls trapped in purgatory was correct.

President Bowman was true to his word. He pulled the scientists out of the secret bunker and had the CDC backup and running within a month. Britton was pleasantly surprised to hear from Adi that one of the scientists working at the CDC was their friend James.

The President started a memorial for all the ill that had disappeared and never came back, as well as for all the missing and presumed dead victims of 2028-45. Britt was instrumental in spearheading the memorial. The names of the known victims were engraved in stone, including her parents and husband. Many of the victims were never identified, including the woman she had befriended. Britt framed and centered the woman's necklace on the memorial as a symbol for the unknown victims, but she secretly hoped someone would recognize it and get some closure she would never have.

"Hello everyone, thank you for tuning into my podcast. My name is Ray and today I have a very special guest. Doctor Britton Gravel. Thank you for coming, Doctor."

"A deal is a deal. Oh, before I forget, thank you for loaning me your book." Britton reached into her bag and slid the Anglo-Saxon dictionary to Ray.

"My pleasure, I hope it came in useful."

"It did, very much. Thank you again."

"Glad to do it. So, it's been one year since you emerged out of the fog, cured the plague and toppled a corrupt government. What have you been up to since then?"

"My biggest goal was to get home and try to get things back to normal for me, my son Hunter and for the people in my home town. I've also been in close contact with Adi..."

"You, of course, mean Mr. Aditya Aggarwal, who is standing right outside the studio window with your son Hunter."

"Yes, that Adi. He has been doing some amazing work helping the other scientists at the CDC to create cures, vaccinations, and antibiotics that are designed to cure even the strongest of bacteria."

"That is excellent. You left out one major accomplishment, you're now a Doctor of Mortuary Sciences."

"That is correct. After struggling with a thesis idea for a long time, I was able to use my experiences with the plague doctors as the foundation."

"That is amazing, congratulations. Speaking of your experience with the plague doctors. That took some serious courage to do what you did, go into the fog with them. Can you tell me a bit about your experiences there?"

Britton went into detail about what she had seen while she was with the doctor. She told Ray how she used his book to communicate, and about her friend. She also showed a picture of the necklace hoping a viewer of the podcast would recognize it.

"That is all absolutely incredible. I couldn't imagine what was going through your head during all that."

"I just kept thinking about my son, about Adi, and about home, but it was definitely an experience I hope to never repeat."

"So, who do you think these doctors are, and where do you think you went?"

"I still don't know, I was hoping you'd be able to tell me," she said with a laugh. "Seriously though, everything I saw and touched all felt very much like I was in the 1300s."

"You believe you went back in time?"

"I'm not saying that. It just felt like that. But after we gave the plague doctor ample supplies of the vaccination Charles and Adi created, many of the victims of our time have returned. But no history books have made any mention of a miracle cure, so I can only assume where Hunter and I went was a spirit world between the living and the dead..."

"Like purgatory?"

"If you like, yes, like purgatory. When our sick were cured, they came home. What I hope is once their sick were treated they were able to cross over to the next realm and finally rest in peace. I also hope once the doctors realize there are no more plague victims, they too will be able to cross over and find the peace they deserve."

"You were able to travel with the plague doctors how?"

"I borrowed an authentic plague doctor suit from the Museum of Oddities in Boston."

"Borrowed?"

"Maybe more aggressively borrowed. I wasn't able to return that suit because the doctors destroyed my old one, but once we got on the same page, they gave me one of theirs, so I was able to give the museum a mint condition suit from that era, almost like it was fresh out of the box. I have since visited the museum and they aren't going to press charges. They say the new suit and story has attracted many new visitors, so all is well."

"That's great, I'm glad they aren't going to throw you in jail. I won't take up any more of your time, doctor. Thank you for joining me on Ray's occult podcast. Please come back and visit us again."

"Absolutely, and thank you for all your help in solving the mystery. We couldn't have done it without you and please, if anyone recognizes the necklace, please let Ray know."

Britt stood up, shook Ray's hand and gave Hunter and Adi a smile before she walked out of the booth to join them.

Author Biography

Ryan L Canning grew up in a small town in Muskoka, Ontario in an artistic environment. Both parents are avid readers and his father was a woodworker. An appreciation for art and the written word were instilled in Ryan at an early age. He explored many different mediums before finding his niche with costume designing and writing. Ryan L Canning has two self-published novels "Syn" and "Synce..." which he wrote under the pseudonym, R.L. Canning. Ryan has taken the lessons he learned writing the 2 full-length novels and applied them to his thriller novella "The Plague."

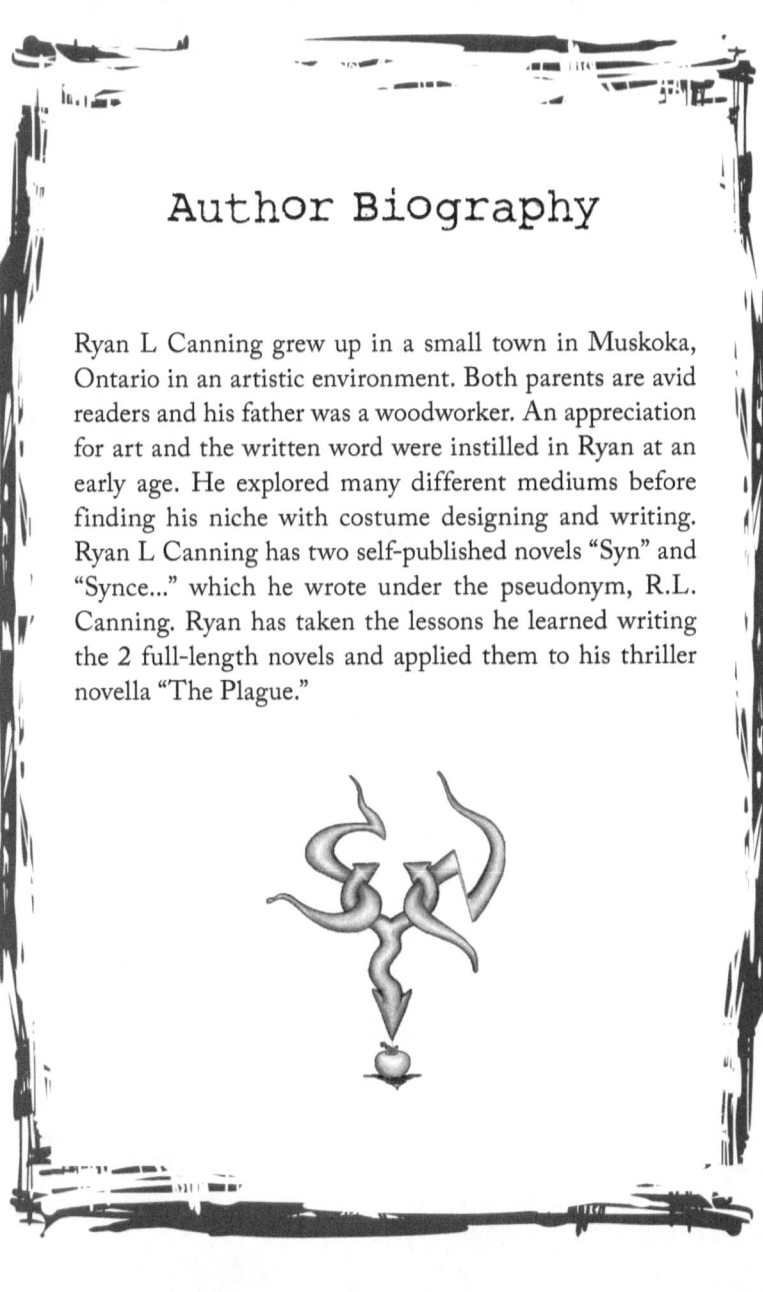

www.ingramcontent.com/pod-product-compliance
Lightning Source LLC
La Vergne TN
LVHW091602060526
838200LV00036B/964
9780228822981